DOWN
TO DARKNESS

Other books by Brian McNaughton

Fiction

The Throne of Bones
Worse Things Waiting
Nasty Stories
Even More Nasty Stories

DOWNWARD TO DARKNESS

Brian McNaughton

WILDSIDE PRESS
Berkeley Heights, New Jersey

Downward to Darkness
A publication of
Wildside Press
P.O. Box 45
Gillette, NJ 07933-0045

www.wildsidepress.com

FIRST EDITION

I had the book that holds the hidden way
Across the void and through the space-hung screens
That hold the undimensioned worlds at bay,
And keep lost aeons to their own demesnes.
— H.P. Lovecraft: "The Fungi from Yuggoth"

Chapter One

*P*atrick Laughlin began to dream about the red-haired woman soon after he and his parents moved into the old mill. In one way, the dreams pleased him. His previous sexual fantasies had revolved around popular actresses, pretty classmates, or strangers glimpsed in crowds. But the red-haired woman was his own creation. He was sure that he had never met anyone like her in waking life, but he knew her features, her gestures, her voice, her personality.

Her personality: that was the catch. He was delighted to have conjured up such a vivid invention, but dismayed by the strange twist his imagination had taken in furnishing her soul. Without warning or apparent reason, she would switch from passion to indifference. She would tempt him, toy with him, mock him. The dreams often frustrated him, and sometimes they scared him. More and more frequently, they disgusted him.

Her name was a mystery. He would know it in the dreams, but it would slither to an inaccessible corner of his mind upon waking. He knew that it was something like Martha or Meredith, but neither was exactly right. Her age was a puzzle, too, but Patrick found it difficult to judge the age of anyone very far removed from his own fifteen years. She was a grown woman, but he could detect no lines around her full mouth, no wrinkles around her dark and deep-set eyes. Her body was provocatively hairless, her skin as smooth and as white as the flesh of an egg.

He knew her body very well indeed. In his fantasies, the girls were shy and demure, succumbing only with reluctance to his irresistible advances. The woman in his dreams flaunted her body, she used it to tease and torment him. She had once ordered him to kiss every inch of it, starting with each toe, not neglecting the spaces between. Having done it, trembling on the brink of consummation, he had woken. He knew that he had woken because she had willed him to.

A man sometimes haunted the dreams, but Patrick knew little about him. He would watch and wait and seem amused by Patrick's torments.

Despite a certain indefinable awkwardness to his gait, he would slip nimbly under the bed, into a closet or through a wall when Patrick tried to confront him. He was a rival, the dreamer know that much, and he hated the elusive figure in black with an intensity that matched his desire for the red-haired woman. In one of the worst dreams, Patrick had stood paralyzed outside the door of a dark room while the man made love to her.

When he was awake, he thought about her constantly. Her character and her appearance were so consistent from night to night and so vivid that he began to believe she must exist in the waking world. He was always on the watch for her, searching the streets, scanning passing cars. Sometimes spotting a slim woman with straight, long hair of a particularly dark-red shade, he would feel a hungry, weightless hollow form inside him, but the ache of exhilaration would fade when a coarse, human face or a graceless, mortal gesture would unmask her as an ordinary woman.

And what could he say to her if he found her in the waking world? She was mature and beautiful and poised and sophisticated. He was even more awkward and shy than most of his contemporaries; he had neither charm nor good looks. Would she know him, would she want to know him, did she share his dreams? He knew that these questions were silly, for she had no life outside his nightmares, but he couldn't stop asking them.

When consciously daydreaming about her, he would try to correct her faults. Listening to Tchaikovsky or Berlioz, he would let himself wander in a world of heroic fantasy where she would be a virginal princess languishing in a wizard's tower. It wouldn't work. She would have no part of it. He would detect that gleam in her deep, dark eyes and know that she herself was more knowing and evil than any wizard he could invent. She would subvert his purity, she would transform his adventure into an orgy.

He couldn't even picture her in different clothes from the ones she always wore. She wore black: severe dresses that brushed the insteps of her black boots, with sometimes a hooded cloak. Her hair would either hang straight down her back like a tail of molten copper or it would be done in braids around her regal little head. She wore no makeup, but the contrast of her white skin, her black eyes and her bright hair against her somber clothes was electrifying.

He no longer slept at night, not as he had once known sleep. He would lie in a feverish state that shifted without clear boundaries between fantasies and dreams. He would flee his bed at first light and seek a book to read, any book, trying to blot her from his mind, until he would hear his mother moving in the kitchen.

It occurred to him that he might be losing his mind. He was certainly obsessed. But he had heard often enough that adolescence was a trial, that chemical changes were going on in his body that could affect his mind.

He had read enough to know that his succubus might be just a surrogate for his mother, his death-pale rival symbolic of his father. He didn't believe that, but he felt that his willingness to consider such explanations was a proof of his sanity. He clung to the hope that his obsession was a state of mind that he would simply outgrow.

He couldn't confide in his parents, because it would then have been necessary to reveal the sexual nature of his dreams. He had never been able to figure out his parents' odd attitude toward his sexual education. They were urbane and sophisticated. His father was a successful commercial artist; his mother had a Ph.D. in English. For as long as he could remember, they had treated him like a miniature adult. Typical of the bedtime stories his mother had read him as a child had been Prescott's *Conquest of Mexico* and Boswell's *Life of Johnson*. His father never toned down a racy anecdote because he was present, nor would his mother expurgate her comments on some friend's love-life. Until a few years ago, his mother had seldom bothered to wear clothes while doing the housework. But he had learned that a simple, direct question about sex could embarrass either of them.

Perhaps what really embarrassed them was the fact of parenthood. They were young, they were free, they had time to conquer the world, but his presence proved that these were delusions. His growth into adolescence signalled their slide into middle age. They preferred to treat him as a young friend who happened to live with them. An archetypal parent-child chat about the birds and the bees would have rubbed their noses in their own mortality. They had always insisted that he call them Frank and Rose.

He had learned about sex by keeping his eyes and ears open at home, by paying attention to the courses at school, by reading the books to which his parents had never denied him access. He knew that his obsession with his fantasy was probably not abnormal, that his indulgence in masturbation was probably not excessive, but it would have been a relief to be able to ask someone the questions and hear the expected answers.

Having reached the limits of knowledge and reason, he was still baffled by one aspect of the dreams. Despite his theoretical grasp of the subject, he had never so much as kissed a girl. Yet the various tastes and smells and textures of the red-haired woman were as real to him in memory as any sensations in the real world. Those rare, blessed occasions on which she had actually let him make love to her had far transcended masturbation or wet dreams. When he would at last succeed in making love to a real person, he knew that the experience would be no different; except, perhaps, that it would not be so good.

From Frank, a vestigial Catholic, he had acquired an obscure and troublesome notion of sin. From reading of gods and heroes in Homer and Malory, he had acquired a notion of pride. Both notions persuaded him that imaginary women and nocturnal emissions were unworthy of him. A real girl was the only cure, and he was ashamed of himself for not getting one. Real girls made him acutely aware that he was too tall and skinny, that his bespectacled eyes were too close together, that his black hair stuck out in odd places, that his hands were too big and bony, that his teeth were crooked. This knowledge tied his tongue. Girls were so smooth and cool and self-contained, when they weren't sniggering at him to his face or whispering about him behind his back. He hated them for making him so aware of his defects, he hated himself for letting them do it. The secret knowledge of his own utter superiority enabled him to defend himself with coldness and sarcasm. He had no friends.

One girl in his class, Shana Jennings, particularly attracted him. Her hair was blond. Her eyes were large and of a particularly light and clear shade of blue. Unlike his succubus, whose nose was long and straight and suggestive of a classical goddess, Shana had a snub nose. Her face was innocent, even vacant and bland. She was a cheerleader, she was a moron, she had tits like melons.

Patrick didn't go to football games, but he liked to watch her at practice, where she would do cartwheels that exposed the bare length of her legs and the snug fit of her underpants. Her legs weren't as long as the red-haired woman's. They were plump, maybe even stubby by comparison. He would often see her with Bruce Curtis, a junior with a wild reputation. Bruce's apelike arm would usually be draped possessively over her shoulders.

One morning she approached him in study period and asked him if he had the answer to a problem in their algebra homework. It turned out that she hadn't done any of the homework at all. He urged her to copy his. Later they whispered about Mr. Bamberger, a teacher they both despised. He was so dazzled by her perspicacity and wit on this subject that he undermined his pose of chilly superiority by giggling and snorting "like a cretin doing barnyard-impersonations," in the words of Ms. Willy, the study-hall monitor. It may have been the first time in high school that a teacher had reprimanded him for anything besides — Mr. Bamberger's words — "a snotty attitude."

After that, Shana always sat beside him at one of the long tables in the rear of the study-hall. He would pass her his homework without making her undergo the embarrassment of asking for it. Exchanging a few words with her would be sufficient repayment for him. He admired her encyclopedic knowledge of pop stars, about whom he knew nothing.

One day, seemingly as absorbed in her copying as a medieval monk, she slipped her foot out of her shoe and began tickling his ankle. He was paralyzed. He dared a sidelong glance at her, her brow furrowed over the work, the tip of her pink tongue protruding slightly from the corner of her mouth in concentration. She didn't know she was touching him: it was just an absent-minded gesture, a nervous tic. She didn't say a word about it when the bell rang and the class dispersed.

He could never initiate such a contact. If he did, she would scream. She wouldn't believe him if he told her she had started it. She wouldn't just slap him, she would get Bruce Curtis to beat him up. But he would be prepared if she did it again. He took special pains to wash his feet and change to fresh socks every morning.

Just as he was beginning to despair, he felt her toes tickling his ankle again. He slipped out of his shoe and responded. She never looked at him; her expression never changed, not even when he twisted his ankle around hers in a way that might have seemed awkward or even painful if it hadn't felt so good. She didn't seem to mind, not even when he screwed up all his courage and put his hand on her thigh. He stared beyond the tables of students at Ms. Willy, absorbed in her copy of *The American Spectator.* He had no idea what to do next. Still scribbling assiduously, Shana took his hand and moved it a little higher.

Then the bell rang, and she was gone. He wanted to pursue her, but he had to wait for a few moments until he had succeeded in willing down his erection.

Unlike his succubus, Shana Jennings was real. Thinking about her was a step toward health and sanity. He needed to make no conscious effort to think about her when he went to bed that night. He thought of her plump legs, her white panties. Peeling them down, she would reveal blond hair, not a bare purse.

He found himself in the vaulted cellar of the mill, as he often did in his dreams. The cellar was more extensive than it was in the real world. He suspected that parts of the real cellar had been bricked up, and that this reflected its original form.

"You can know that saucy jolthead if you wish."

They sat on opposite sides of a table, and a feast lay between them. He sat sideways, unwilling to look at her or acknowledge her remark. He was unaccountably reluctant to look at the food, too, although his mouth watered from the strong smell of roast meat in his nostrils. He grew more and more ravenous.

"There be spells to ensure a wench's complaisance, but none more effective than a brick, wrapped in a sock." Her voice was a purr that mocked tenderness. "Do you fear my jealousy?"

He jerked front to face her. How could he have compared her to Shana Jennings? The comparison was not just absurd, it was blasphemous. This was the most desirable woman who had ever lived.

"You're not afraid to make me jealous." He meant it to be a snarl, but it came out as a whine.

She laughed.

"That man —"

She interrupted: "Is yourself. He is your shadow. When you refuse to stand in the light, your shadow falls in odd places."

"This is crazy. But since it's my dream, I guess *I'm* crazy."

"You're hungry."

"I couldn't. I can't." He shuddered. "No, not even in a dream, this. . . . Why do you make me do these things?"

"To strengthen you for that which must be done." Her dark eyes seemed to bore into his brain. "Why do you fight me? Don't you want me? Don't you want to join your own shadow in my embrace?"

His hunger became a pain that kept him from speaking or even thinking. He tore at the meat on the table and crammed a wad into his mouth. Juice and fat ran down his chin as he chewed the crackling flesh.

"The plump little piglet called Shana is but the least of the prizes you may win if you stop resisting and receive the light."

She shamed him by taking up her knife and fork and carving daintily. He felt like a gross buffoon. She often made him feel like that. She extended a bit of meat on the fork and let him take it between his lips. He stared at her as he chewed, desiring her with all his soul but content, for the moment, to be with her and be fed choice tidbits like a pampered pet.

Patrick woke. The memory of the dream racked him with nausea beyond endurance. He ran to the bathroom and retched over the toilet. Although his stomach heaved and churned, he could not eject its vile burden. He ran water into his cupped hand and drank, trying to wash away the memory of the taste. He scrubbed his face and hands three times over, but they still felt slimed with the obscene grease.

Before leaving the bathroom, he remembered to wash his feet.

Downstairs, his mother was just beginning to cook breakfast. She was a thin woman. Wearing his father's bathrobe, she seemed even slighter in the gloomy cavern of the oversized kitchen. The noise of the millrace outside was loud. It had been loud in the dream, too. The inessential details of the dreams came perilously close to reality.

"Good morning," she said. "You sleep well?"

He grunted.

"How do you want your eggs?"

"I don't want any, thank you."

"Well, what would you like?"

He said nothing as he poured coffee and sweetened it with honey. Rose believed that sugar caused cancer. When he went to the refrigerator for skim milk, he selected an assortment of vitamins and herbal extracts from six different bottles in the hope it would keep her from pressing him to eat.

"Cereal?" she suggested. "Fruit?"

"My stomach feels funny," he said, sitting at the wide-planked table and stirring his coffee.

She turned to study him. Her dark hair, pulled back from her angular face, held streaks of gray that she didn't try to conceal. Dark smudges showed under her eyes.

"Your stomach *looks* funny. Six-foot-three, and I bet you don't weigh eighty pounds. You're going to make yourself very sick indeed if you don't eat."

He pushed the pills around the table in random patterns to draw her attention to them. She abandoned the stove and joined him with her coffee. She had freckles and prominent upper teeth. He had once heard someone describe her as *handsome,* a word that struck him as odd but just.

"It's this fucking barn we live in," she said. "It's a wonder we don't all have bubonic plague. Maybe we do."

She surprised him. She used indelicate words only when a subject moved her strongly, and she had never expressed dissatisfaction with the mill before.

"Something wrong?" He was glad to turn the conversation away from himself.

She lit a cigarette. She believed that they caused cancer, too, but sugar was easier to give up. A persistent clacking of crows outside distracted her, and she turned to scream, "Fly south, you bastards, why don't you?"

"I don't think they ever do."

"That's only one of the things we should have looked into before we moved here. Have you ever noticed," she said slowly, "that the millrace sounds like voices?"

He was caught off guard. He had thought that was one of the symptoms of his own disorder. He was afraid that his panic showed, but she stared moodily at the blue coils of cigarette smoke rising into the dusty sunlight.

"Yes. At night. Sometimes."

She nodded. "Exactly. Now, for instance, it just sounds like water gurgling." She stopped and listened as if to prove this to herself. "But at night. . . . Last night I could have sworn that two people under the window were holding a conversation that I couldn't quite make out. Whispering and chuckling and going on and on."

"I've heard it sound like that. Sometimes." He found that he could swallow the pills and the coffee.

"Last night it got to the point where I couldn't stand it anymore. I got up and looked out the window. I still heard them, and for a moment I thought I saw someone. I went out and walked around the pond. I finally convinced myself that it was only the splashing of the water. But it wasn't easy."

"You saw someone?"

"I thought I did. For a moment. I thought it was you, only. . . . It was no one, of course, only a shadow."

Patrick had never tried to persuade himself that it wasn't the red-haired woman's voice that he heard. It always sounded like her voice, the sense of the words shifted ever-so-slightly out of reach by the noise of running water.

"It's easy to see how legends of dryads got started," she said.

"You mean, *naiads*. Dryads live in trees."

"You're right, of course." She frowned, and he heard Mr. Bamberger lecturing him about his "snotty attitude." He ought to go easier on his own mother. She said, "I think the damned naiads have been giving me nightmares."

"*Naiadmares.*" What he had intended as a quip came out sounding so gloomy and portentous that he shivered. He didn't dare reveal his eagerness to hear about her nightmares.

Her appreciative chuckle was mirthless. "Maybe our naiad objected to having her creek dammed up and forced to run a mill, and now, after a hundred and fifty years, she's at last got some poor suckers to get even with." She jolted him with an unexpected question: "Have you been sleeping well?"

He looked away, shrugging. He was on the very brink of pouring out a complete and honest answer, when she continued: "I dream about the cellar all the time, the God-damned cellar. I suppose that's logical. The cellar is below the level of the pond, isn't it? So it would be the part of the house most vulnerable to a water-spirit. It always seems — in these dreams, that is — that there's something buried in the cellar, something that will make me rich and powerful and young if I dig it up. Then I can have everything I ever saw in the movies."

He laughed aloud at this allusion to one of their favorite films, but her smile was only a perfunctory flicker as she pressed on: "Like the Rhinegold. Whoever gave up love and forged the Rhinegold into a ring would become master of the universe. Except that it was a dirty trick, there was a curse on it, and it brought about the end of the world. "I suppose the Rhine maidens who guarded it technically qualify as naiads, don't they?"

"What does she look like?"

"Who?"

"The naiad."

"Oh, don't listen to me, I'm talking nonsense. It's only a dream."

He wasn't convinced by her laugh, her sudden shift of mood, but he could think of no effective way of questioning her without telling her too much.

"I've made you late. You'll miss the schoolbus if you don't get out of here right now."

He got up to kiss her, and her forehead felt clammy to his lips. Under his hand, her shoulder was stiff and tense.

He had forgotten to do his algebra homework, and Shana Jennings was furious. He tried to do it in study period while she seethed and fidgeted beside him, but he couldn't concentrate. When the bell rang and she flounced out without speaking to him, he hardly noticed. He was thinking of his mother, walking out into the moonlight and straining to discern ghostly voices through the gurgle of the millrace.

He wondered if it were possible for a mother and son to develop, independently of each other, a strikingly similar form of madness.

But even his concern for Rose was secondary to the question gnawing relentlessly at his mind. He wondered whether he could find the answer in some early explorer's memoirs or in an anthropological treatise.

He wondered whether such books could tell him if young, tender pork was similar to the flesh of a baby.

Chapter Two

*I*f Frank Laughlin had been given a choice, he would have picked Wagnerian opera as the last thing he wanted to blast him out of a sound sleep. Then again, maybe that choice wouldn't even have occurred to him, because no human being could be so perverse and diabolical as to wake up a fellow creature that way. Rose couldn't be doing it. She couldn't. The Nazis must have come back and taken over during the night. Heinrich Himmler was waiting to interrogate him in the living room.

"Jesus fucking Christ!" he screamed.

Screaming was futile. Rose was getting every penny's worth of amplification from the expensive stereo. Frank picked up the bedside table and pounded its legs against the floor. Even that did no good. Undisturbed, Brunhilde howled her farewells as Valhalla went up in musical flames.

"Motherfucking bastard bitch cunt!" Frank roared as he launched himself toward the bedroom door. He collided with the jamb, spun, half-fell down the stairs. He had to force himself to enter the living room, because the volume of sound had passed the threshold of pain. He snapped off the set and leaned on it for a moment, gasping for breath. His ears rang.

Rose wasn't even in the room. Of course not. As any sensible person would, she had gone to the next county to listen. He went to the sideboard and sloshed vodka into a glass. Only when it was burning its way down his gullet did he realize what he was doing. She had literally driven him to drink.

"Rose!"

She drifted into the room. Her appearance, pale and distraught, took some of the edge off his fury.

"I'm sorry. I guess it was too loud?"

"Yeah, you might say that. You might say it was loud. That would be a reasonable statement. You could also say Shakespeare was an adequate playwright or that the universe contains several stars."

"Did you have to turn it off?" She drifted toward the stereo.

"No, of course I didn't have to turn it off. I could have stayed in bed while my teeth rattled loose from my skull and the sound-waves melted my bones and I dissolved into a mindless, whimpering puddle of jelly. But if you turn it on again, I'll break your fucking arm."

She turned away from the set and sat down. She didn't look at him. Her shoulders were hunched, her head bowed. "The noise of the water was getting on my nerves," she said.

He took several deep breaths and a long drink of the vodka. "I'm sorry. I didn't mean that, you know it. I'm not at the top of my form when I wake up. You know that."

"I was being selfish. I wanted you up. I didn't want to be alone, listening to the water."

"Yeah, it can get on your nerves, I guess. It's nice at night, though. It puts me to sleep. But next time you want me to get up, do it more gently, like setting fire to the bed, okay?"

She giggled, and he assumed his apology had been accepted. He freshened his drink and sat on the couch beside her.

"Christ. This is the earliest I ever started drinking in my entire life. I'm not even awake. Maybe I'll go back to bed. What's wrong with a Mozart quintet? Does it have to be Wagner? What time is it? Would you get some ice?"

She took his glass and went to the kitchen. She wore a garish, bandanna-patterned blouse, a pair of tan jeans that hugged her trim buttocks intriguingly. He leaned forward, large elbows on large knees, and rubbed his large face. The position made him aware of his large belly. Odd that he should have married a skinny woman and gotten such a skinny kid. Patrick had inherited his looks entirely through Rose. He looked just like youthful photographs of her crazy father, whose memory she venerated to a degree that Frank sometimes thought unwholesome.

Slightly repentant, he lowered the volume control on the stereo and turned it back on. Brunhilde groaned like a resuscitated dinosaur, rapidly gathered momentum, was soon singing in her proper key. He studied the cover of the album, which had been around forever. It featured a murky painting by Ryder that had always given him the creeps. He wondered if Rose's crazy father had given it to her. Her dowry.

"Thank you," she said, returning with his glass. "I was in the mood for it, that's all. To answer your other question, it's eleven o'clock."

"It's time I was up. I have to call Roberts. He's busting my ass this month. When did they make the law that all art-directors have to be vicious little nitpicking faggots? What was the word he used? *Sinister.* He says my work has become sinister, for Christ's sake, and that's not going to sell lemon-scented douchebags or whatever the fuck they're trying to sell. I can't even think this morning."

"I can't imagine you being sinister even if you tried."

"It's nice of you to say that, but it's not really a compliment. I'm a pro, I can be anything I want to be, and if Roberts wanted sinister, he'd get sinister. Only that's not what he's getting, the sniveling fairy, he's getting what he asked for, but it probably gives him a delicious little sexual *frisson* to play Pope Whozis to my Michelangelo."

"Maybe it's this house. This house is sinister."

"Oh, bullshit, you don't understand what I'm saying." He got up and paced the room. The music made him restless and irritable, but he couldn't turn it off now. Rose had a gift for maneuvering him into untenable positions. His anger at being woken by that godawful noise had been perfectly justified, but he had overreacted, as she had known he would. She had wanted him awake, she had wanted to hear Wagner, and now she had both; and the guilt was all his. Compounding his guilt, he was getting drunk before breakfast in a gaudy set of striped pajamas. He poured more vodka over his ice.

She was too smart for her own good. So was Patrick, and that was a damned shame. She had seen how smart he was, how much like her he was, and she had pushed him too far too early. She had raised him to believe that he could do anything because he was a genius, and now he couldn't even get a date. Simple contentment was a high enough goal for any man, Frank believed, and God knew it was tough enough to get even that. He would have been satisfied with a son who wanted to spend his life as a supermarket bagboy, as long as the son would have been happy with such a life. Instead, thanks to Rose, he had Lord Byron, without the title, the money, the looks or the talent. With only the sulks, the moods, the poses and the arrogance of the poet, Patrick was doomed.

The music ended, but Frank's spirits didn't lift. He watched how Rose ballooned the paper sleeve of the record deftly with one hand, held the record in the other so that her fingers never touched the grooves. She did the little things like that flawlessly, never even needing to think about them. It was only on the big things, like raising a son, that she screwed up. He sighed. That really wasn't her fault, either. Struggling to build a career, he had scarcely noticed Patrick for the first fifteen years of his life.

"Are you ready for breakfast?"

"Does that mean, have I stopped drinking?"

"Of course not."

"Yes. Yes, I would like some. Thanks." Maybe she was right about the house. He seemed to be reading sinister meanings into everything she said lately.

"Mix me a bloody, and I'll join you," she said.

He brought the bottle with him as he followed her through the enormous room they facetiously called the Great Hall. Floored with massive planks intended to support heavy machinery, it rose to the full height of the mill. They both loved its baronial scale, but they had yet to think of an everyday use for it. Rose had decorated it with some of Frank's watercolors, but they seemed pathetically few and small.

They went on to the kitchen, a room he disliked. The stone walls were a foot thick. What little light penetrated the small, inset windows had been reflected from the algae-scummed pond outside, producing odd glimmers and ripples in unexpected corners. The brass gleam of pots and pans hanging from a thick beam suggested the obscure tools of a creative inquisitor. An iron maiden wouldn't have looked out of place in one of the gloomier corners. Instead, there was the Cuisinart.

He assembled the ingredients and mixed her a bloody mary, refilling his own glass and tinting it with tomato juice. He and Rose had worked together on plans for modernizing the mill, but the kitchen was the only room that conformed entirely with her ideas. Parts of the house were futuristic, others were an uneasy compromise with the original contours, but the kitchen was solidly rooted in the past. When called upon to praise their house, friends usually chose the word "interesting."

"When you call Roberts, why don't you invite him to the party?"

"Hallowe'en is his national holiday. He'll be prancing down Christopher Street in his gold lamé leotard."

"It won't hurt to ask him. It might even do some good, if you can restrain yourself for one night from telling fag-jokes."

"He likes fag-jokes," Frank grumbled. "Are you really going to invite Howie?"

She set his bacon and eggs before him and took a sip of her drink. At last she shrugged and said, "You know him, I don't. What do you think?"

"It's a big day for him, too. It would be like asking the pope to an egg-hunt on Easter Sunday."

"But Hallowe'en is really on a Tuesday, and the party will be the Saturday before. I forgot toast. Do you want some?"

He did, but he decided against it. Bacon and eggs were bad enough. He had to do something about his weight. The two flights to his studio made him short of breath. He recalled how he had once planned to jog around the pond every morning before breakfast. In the two months since they'd moved in, he hadn't even walked around the pond.

He was still hungry when he finished, but he shoved the plate aside as decisively as if it held all his bad habits. "Anyway," he said, reaching for one of Rose's cigarettes, "if you're used to drinking bats' blood and eviscerating virgins, you won't get off on popping party-favors and shouting, 'Whee!'"

"I'll tell him he doesn't have to shout 'Whee!' if he doesn't want to. I'm sure he doesn't really do all those other things."

"He tries to encourage the impression that he does. It might ruin his reputation if it got around that he went to a bourgeois Hallowe'en party dressed as Kermit the Frog." He paused to cough and sip his drink. "Yeah, let's invite him, what the hell, he'll be a conversation-piece. Christ, a costume-party. The whole thing seems too Scott-and-Zelda-ish in the cold light of day."

"We can't back out. I've asked too many people."

The note of regret in her voice surprised him. The party had been her idea, and she had pushed it with enthusiasm.

"What about your friend with the shiny nose?"

"After the twentieth time, that joke loses some of its charm."

He thought of humming the tune of his parody, "Rupert the Rotten Writer," but he restrained himself. He supposed he really was jealous of Rupert Spencer, who was fifteen years younger than he and looked — to quote another joke he had overused — like a handsome version of Robert Redford. Rupert came to Rose ostensibly for criticism of his scribblings, and he would gaze at her like a homeless puppy while she scanned them.

"How about Mrs. Minotaur?" he asked.

She flicked her hand in exasperation. "I wish you wouldn't make up silly names for everyone we know. I'm sure I'll slip one of these days and call her that. And Howard Ashcroft isn't really called Howie, is he?"

"God, no. Dr. Ashcroft, but I don't know what he's a doctor of. Maybe he'll be impressed enough to come if you sign yourself Dr. Laughlin."

"Maybe he can exorcise this place."

Her intensity startled him. Something was obviously bothering her. First the Wagner, then the indifference to the party, now this cryptic remark. Whatever it was, he didn't feel up to dealing with it now. As he often told himself, she was probably just getting her period.

"Howie works the other side of the street," he said. "If the house bugs you that much, you might ask him to have it split in two and fall into the tarn."

She didn't elaborate on her complaint with the house. Instead, she said, "What about Patrick?"

"I suppose we can't get out of inviting *him.*"

"What I mean is, shouldn't we suggest that he invite some of his friends?"

He ignored that loaded question, sipping his drink.

"I know he's always acted just like another adult at our parties, but he's at the age when he'd probably prefer to be with his contemporaries. He's been growing a little distant lately." She brooded for a moment. "He might prefer to host a sort of teenage annex to the party, here in the kitchen or somewhere. Can you think of any people who might have kids his age?"

He was relieved by her last question. It showed that she recognized the existence of the problem, even if she was unwilling to admit outright that Patrick had no friends.

"I don't know. Bill and Carla, of course. Mrs. Minotaur has a daughter, doesn't she? God knows how. And I don't know who else, I guess you could ask around. Maybe Howie has some virgins in his basement that he doesn't need to sacrifice right away. They'd probably welcome a night out." He couldn't resist adding: "And of course Rupert will be here, he's in Patrick's age group."

"I might just run away with him, you bastard. That would take some of the edge off your wit."

He reached out and placed his hand over hers on the table. "That's what I'm afraid of, of course," he said, his tone a study in earnestness. "I love you, pinhead."

She lowered her head and smiled, tight-lipped, as she returned the pressure of his hand.

"Let's go back to bed," he suggested.

As if on cue, the doorbell rang before she could answer. Chances were it was Rupert or Carla Kraft or Mrs. Minotaur, here for an extended natter. Whoever it was, he didn't want to confront them at noon in his circus-striped pajamas. He kissed Rose lightly on the lips and retreated.

In his studio, after catching his breath, Frank dialed Alfred Roberts. He was put on hold and forced to listen to a tape of Italo-American ballads for five minutes, a torment that Dante hadn't thought of. After that, if Roberts spoke one discouraging word, Frank vowed to drive to New York and fling him out his twentieth-story window. But Roberts disarmed him completely.

"Frank, this is marvelous! This is precisely what I've been badgering you for, I'm just overwhelmed. Where on earth did you find such an absolutely exquisite model?"

"They're a dime a dozen up here, Alfred, you really have to come and check out the local supply of cunt."

"No *thank* you. I have my hands full as it is. It still looks terribly . . . no, not sinister anymore, the word has to be *outré*, but of course you know that."

"Of course," he said, wondering if Rose would know what that meant.

"The *farouche* quality of those deep-set eyes . . . the bone-structure . . . it's almost as if I were looking at a beautiful skull. I've never said it to a straight person before, Frank, but you're a genius."

"I'm yours, you silver-tongued devil."

"Oh, Frank, if only that were true!" he sighed. Switching abruptly to his all-business tone, he added, "When can you give me the rest of it?"

"I can bring it down the first of the week, I guess. Okay? Listen, Alfred, before you hang up, my wife and I are throwing a Hallowe'en party, a costume party, a week from Saturday. We'd be delighted to have you."

"Well. . . ."

"We have a lot of interesting people, believe it or not, including a certified Satanist. Only thing is, you can't come as Kermit the Frog, that's taken."

"Actually, I think I'd like to come. May I bring a friend?"

"Of course, bring several, the more the gayer — er, I mean, the *merrier.*"

"Who writes your material, Frank, Jerry Falwell?"

"It's a big house, we have room for any number of people to stay over."

"It sounds wonderful, Frank. I'm really glad you asked me. I've just been dying to see how you rate as an interior decorator."

"Great. Give my love to the gang at the Mine Shaft, Alfie."

"Frank, you're such a thoroughly despicable swine that it's almost refreshing to talk to you. And, Frank? I have a super idea for your Hallowe'en costume if you haven't decided yet."

"Yes?"

"The ghost of Mama Cass," Roberts said, and he quickly hung up.

Frank laughed as he dropped the receiver. He had been thinking of dressing as W.C. Fields, whom he saw as a kindred spirit, but maybe he would follow Roberts's suggestion. No, he'd better not. Artsy-craftsy though the community of Mt. Tabor might be, the conspicuous presence of Roberts and his cronies — and how many had his expansive invitation just let him in for? — would cause a little talk. If, in addition, the host were in drag, the talk would never stop; and its ultimate victim would be Patrick. His son had enough problems without a transvestite father to live down.

He went and changed to his work-clothes, a pair of jeans that the Ramones would have discarded and a Syracuse University sweatshirt. He hadn't gone to Syracuse, he'd gone to Harvard, but he cherished the shirt as a badge of reverse snobbery. He put on his paint-spattered Mets cap and began the automatic preparation of his tools.

What a nasty and complicated and unforgiving place the world was! Roberts was a handsome and talented and intelligent young man, with about five-hundred years of experience lurking in his innocent green eyes. Yet he had invited this seductive basilisk into his own home, where he would meet his confused and unsophisticated son. He couldn't rescind the invitation. For one thing, he liked Roberts; for another, he was money in the bank.

He decided he was borrowing trouble. Patrick's head was on straight. Roberts would respect the obligations of a guest. Christ! He was thinking like a father forced by circumstance to introduce his daughter to Casanova. Bob Dylan hadn't just been whistling "Dixie," and the times had certainly changed. If he wanted something to worry about, he could examine his own curious habit of flirting with Roberts, most often from the impersonal safety of a telephone.

But self-examination had never been his style. He felt more comfortable with his sudden surge of resentment toward Rose. According to the explanation Frank believed, a homosexual rejects his coarse, crude father as a role-model and turns to someone softer and sweeter and more congenial to emulate: his mother. Rose had actively encouraged that dislocation of Patrick's bearings. In more ways than one, she had tried to seduce his son away from him. With infinite patience and love, she had opened to him the treasures of the intellectual world. While other kids stumbled laboriously over the hard words in the adventures of Dick and Jane, Patrick had been breezing through Gibbon. And she had opened her heart to him. They shared a bond of confidence and closeness that he could never hope to penetrate.

More than that, she had admitted him to the mysteries of her body. There they had sprawled, on the floor before the fireplace in their Chelsea walk-up, mother and son, the mother reading poetry aloud: a picture that would have got Norman Rockwell all choked up. Except that the mother and ten-year-old son had both been bald-ass naked; except that the son had been fondling the mother's tits with a weird mixture of curiosity and affection and excitement; except that the mother, reading on in her well-modulated Vassar voice as if oblivious to his questing hands, had been obviously aroused.

He should have put a stop to it long before it reached that stage, when he had taken Rose aside and quietly promised to blast her teeth through her asshole if she ever pulled anything remotely like that again. Well, he had tried to put a stop to it on previous occasions. He used to object to her taking showers with Patrick when the boy was five or six; but she had ripped him up and down with such calm, condescending scorn that he had held his peace for too long. He was, she told him, a sick, repressed, puritanical, bigoted bog-trotter, a figure of fun in the world of real people, a man so far out of touch with his emotions that he could only get it up on Saturday night with the lights out: a description that came close enough to the truth to be painful. But she would raise her son as a Child of Nature without crippling inhibitions.

Frank had acquiesced merely to avoid tiresome arguments — the story of his life — until he found them that night before the fire. He had never struck her, and he believed he never could, but his threat must have conveyed passionate conviction, because she changed her ways, at least in respect to casual nudity. But she still treated Patrick less like a son than a suitor. And now the Child of Nature had become a jittering twitch.

Dogs barked in his yard. He didn't need to go to the window to confirm that the caller was Mrs. Minotaur, but he went and looked anyway. He saw what he had expected, a black Bronco in the drive and a pack of obstreperous and ill-assorted hounds frolicking in the yard. Minotaur was the perfect name for their *Mumsy*: the mythical creature with the body of a man and the head of a bull.

At least it wasn't Rupert. It annoyed him to have Rupert mooning around downstairs when he was trying to work, even though he trusted that Rose had more sense than to succumb to his blandishments. Even if she did succumb, she would have more sense than to run off with him. For a moment his attitude made him feel terribly urbane and sophisticated, even continental; but he know on brief reflection that his pose wouldn't have survived real proof of infidelity.

He sang softly:

Rupert the Rotten Writer wrote some really rotten prose,
And if you ever read it, you would almost say it blows.

It certainly needed work, he was willing to admit that much.

He returned to his easel and studied the sinuous contours of the woman Roberts had praised. Where, indeed, had he got the model? He wished he knew. Give him a crack at this one, and he would have given Rose a blank check for all the Ruperts she wanted. He had used his photo file when he'd started on the series of illustrations, but the woman had come out looking like none of the photographs.

After Roberts had called the pictures "sinister," he had made one simple change, and everything had fallen into place. From that point, his hand had moved as if it were guided. The change he'd made was to give her red hair.

Chapter Three

*J*ane Miniter always looked as if she'd just tramped in from a day's rough shooting on the moors. Commenting on the tweed scuttle that was habitually jammed down on her brows, Frank had said that an Irishman would one day be canonized for chasing all the silly hats out of his country. Her Norfolk jacket boasted a dominatrix's ransom of superfluous buckles and pockets and leather patches. Her skirt had been woven from a double thickness of burlap and twigs. Her waffle-soled shoes had been designed by Martians for a lifetime of hard use, and she walked as if she were squashing bugs. She seemed incomplete without a shotgun cradled on her arm, but she would never have owned one. Her hobby was writing letters to the local weekly newspaper, denouncing guns and hunters and calling on the government to seize both.

"Hello, Rose. You don't mind if I come in and visit, do you? I was passing by on my way from town. Is it all right if I let the boys out? They could use a romp."

She didn't wait for an answer, but stomped back to her Bronco and flung the doors wide, bellowing encouragement to the pack that boiled forth. They were of many colors and sizes. Frank said they were purebred Polish shepherds.

"I'm glad you dropped by. I wanted to talk to you about the party," Rose said when Jane returned and squeezed through the door, pushing back the canine mass that tried to follow. "Would you like a drink, or shall I make tea?"

"I need a drink. You wouldn't believe the kind of morning I've had. I'll take scotch if you've got it."

Jane followed her to the kitchen and slumped heavily at the table. "Make it a good, stiff belt." She extracted a blue pack of Gauloises from one of her innumerable pockets. "It's really been one of those days."

"I wanted to ask you to bring Amy to the party," Rose hastened to say before Jane could get launched on an account of her day, which would leave no question unanswered about what she had eaten for breakfast, which pair of underpants she had chosen to wear, how long her shower had taken, and exactly what sort of health and mood she and Amy and each of the dogs were experiencing. This Minotaur carried her own labyrinth around with her in the form of her conversation. Rose would have to remember that quip for Frank.

"Thanks," Jane said, taking the drink. "What on earth do you want Amy for? She'd put a damper on anyone's party."

"Jane, that's terrible! Your own daughter —"

"Well, it's the truth. She's a mope. Having her mother drag her along to a grown-ups' party would just underline the fact that she doesn't have a hope in hell of getting a date on a Saturday night."

"I just thought it would be nice for Patrick to have some people his own age here."

"He doesn't have a date either, huh?"

"That isn't it at all." Rose struggled to conceal her irritation. "He wouldn't want to miss the party, and I want him here. Frank is inviting all sorts of artistic people from New York, and we're even going to invite Dr. Ashcroft, to make it a *real* Hallowe'en party."

"Oh, God, I just sicced the cops on Ashcroft. Maybe I'd better not come."

"What do you mean?"

"Well." Jane paused to ignite her Zippo and exhale a cloud of acrid smoke. "I decided to make pancakes and sausages this morning, and that takes a little time, because as I've told you, I don't get this commercial brown-'n'-serve muck, I always get the homemade ones from Fliegler's, and it's wise to parboil them for ten or fifteen minutes before you brown them. You can't be too —"

"Jane —"

"I'm coming to the point, but this is important. Anyway, I never let the boys run loose in the morning because we live so near the highway, and so they just had to wait until I'd made breakfast and could go out with them. I had to do that first, of course, so Amy wouldn't be late for school. She wound up not going to school at all, as it turned out"

"Jane, you were going to tell me about Dr. Ashcroft."

"That's *exactly* what I'm getting to. Give me a refill, huh? Thanks. Anyway, Bozo just won't wait. He's becoming incontinent in his old age, but fortunately he's also old enough to have the sense not to get run over by some idiot barreling through from Massachusetts. So I had to let him out by himself. It was either that, or swab the decks after him, and he's been troubled with diarrhea lately."

Seeing that protest was futile, Rose got up and mixed herself a second bloody mary, even though she had planned on limiting herself to one. She had accepted the first one only to keep Frank company, but now she needed the second.

"The rest of the boys were really put out over that. It's incredible, the sense of justice and fair play that these supposedly lower animals have, and any hint that one of them is being treated like a privileged character sparks a mutiny in the ranks. Lance tried to get even by swiping the sausages right out of the hot frying pan, even though that's the last thing Lance would ever do under normal circumstances, but I turned my back on him for a minute, and there he was with his monster paws up on the stove. I caught him in time, and you can believe I gave him the scolding of his young life."

"Lance is a collie, isn't he?" Rose asked out of sheer perversity.

"No, no, no, that's Dougall, and he isn't a collie at all, he's a highland sheepdog. Lance is a Doberman, although he doesn't look like it, because I think it's cruel and unnatural to dock a dog's tail or crop his ears, so he consequently has floppy ears and a long, ratty tail, but I'm sure he's happier that way and quite thoroughly satisfied with his own good looks. Where was I?"

"You were scolding Lance." Rose added a touch of vodka to her drink. "For trying to steal the sausages. The home-made ones, from Fliegler's."

"Yes, of course, and that's when Amy came downstairs and asked me what was the matter with Bozo. She —"

Indulging her fit of masochism to the hilt, Rose asked: "What kind of dog is Bozo?"

"You know very well, Rose, he's the big tan one, half boxer and half golden retriever. He gets his size from the retriever and his massiveness and short hair from the boxer. Only now he's getting cysts under his coat, and he's not as playful as he used to be, but — oh, this is really quite beside the point, you shouldn't sidetrack me like this! Anyway, Amy asked me what was the matter with Bozo, he was howling beside the brook. I hadn't heard a thing, the boys in the kitchen were making such a racket, I think they were all siding with Lance and telling me how unfair I'd been. He wasn't making a sound himself, just sulking under the table and looking terribly put-upon. I told Amy to keep her eye on the sausages while I went out on the porch and called Bozo, but he just wouldn't come. That isn't like him at all, although he *is* hard of hearing, but he actually looked at me when I called, so I knew he heard me perfectly well. But my point is, it was terribly fortunate that Bozo was out there alone to find it, just because I decided to make pancakes and sausages. They're all good boys, but I know what they're capable of, and I think some of them — like Marcel, for instance, he has no sense of decency — would have snatched it up and run off with it, even if I'd been there."

"Snatched what up? What did he find?"

"That's what I'm trying to tell you. I was in quite a quandary, standing there in my robe and slippers. I didn't want to put on a show for the neighbors by wading down to the brook in that outfit, but Bozo obviously wanted me to come. Oh, Rose, it was *horrible!*"

Rose was shaken by the agony in Jane's eyes, by the sudden draining of color from her face. She had been more roundabout than usual in coming to her point, apparently because the point had profoundly upset her. Rose reached across the table and took her hands.

"It was a baby, Rose," she whispered, "a little baby girl."

"Oh, no! Why is there so much of that lately, irresponsible kids who'd rather kill their children than own up to —"

"It wasn't like that, Rose, not at all. This baby had been burned and mutilated. I took Bozo by the collar — he was every bit as upset as myself, he loves children — and ran to the Baxters' house to call the police, so as not to upset Amy. I had to tell her, of course, but I wanted to do it in my own time, after notifying the police as quickly as possible. It's incredible how imperceptive some people can be; it seemed like it took twenty minutes before Jill Baxter could grasp that I needed to use her phone. Meanwhile, of course, the boys were back home, clamoring to be let out, and I was afraid that Amy might take them out without knowing — but fortunately she didn't, and I finally got through to Chief Marlowe. Isn't that ludicrous? A Keystone Kop named Philip Marlowe. Raymond Chandler must twirl in his grave every time that fool leaves his office to bungle a nuisance-call. But that was only the beginning of my ordeal."

Rose knew that it was only the beginning of hers, too. She poured more vodka into her glass and gestured for Jane to help herself to the scotch.

"I don't know whether I did right in keeping Amy home from school, but I just couldn't bear the thought of being alone. Perhaps I was being selfish, because she's not doing as well in school as she should, and the main reason seems to be her chronic absenteeism. She gets every bug that comes along, and they seem to hit her harder than they do anyone else, even though everyone in my family has been healthy as a horse. I think that Arnold, my late husband —"

"Who was the baby? Where did it come from?"

"Well, this is where the story would become downright ridiculous, if it weren't painful. As soon as Fearless Fosdick had heard my story, he started to ask me all sorts of questions about poor Amy. And then he actually had the nerve to start questioning Amy herself, before it dawned on me what sort of evil little bee he had in his bonnet. Perhaps I am being a little less than fair to him. You jumped to the conclusion yourself that an unwed mother left it, probably a teen-ager. And if you find a dead baby in a young girl's backyard, I suppose it's only natural to ask her a few questions — but *Amy!* Really, Rose, if a boy so much as said hello to her, she'd scream and run home to hide under the bed."

"Well, it's often the shy ones — I mean, I can understand how he might — it's his job, after all." Rose marveled at her own talent for putting her foot in her mouth so thoroughly.

"I know what you're saying, of course, but I also know that Amy had the curse ten days ago. She's so disorganized that buying sanitary napkins at the last minute is one of the continuing crises at our house. Anyway, that's all beside the point. Assuming it had been Amy's baby, which it wasn't, do you suppose she would have cooked it and half-eaten it?"

"Oh, God."

Jane nodded vigorously. "That was the very description of the crime given by our local soul of tact and delicacy, Chief Philip 'I-Am-The-Law' Marlowe. My God, Rose, do you realize how sensitive she is? Do you suppose she'll ever get over it? Being accused of murdering and cannibalizing a child? Oh, it makes me so angry . . . so sick. . . ."

Jane's eyes misted. She squeezed them shut and shook her head violently. Rose had never seen her cry. She had never before heard her express any affection for her daughter, either. She had always regarded Jane as a colorful caricature, an eccentric to be cultivated as a source of anecdotes to tell Frank. Now she felt a surge of warmth toward her and a sense of shame for her own shallowness.

"I suppose I should go back to her now," Jane said. "I shouldn't have left her at all, but I was so angry I went into town to talk to George Spencer, to see if I could sue that dumb prick for his insinuations. George told me I can't; a policeman is apparently free to suspect anyone of anything, however wrong-headedly, and ask any sort of question, however vicious and stupid."

"He doesn't *suspect* her! Not still!"

"No, of course not, he even made a very pretty apology with his hat in his hand. 'You have to excuse me for pillaging your town and raping your women, but, as Attila the Hun, it's my duty.' I was sorely tempted to tell Lance that Philip Marlowe was a bad man."

"I'm sorry, I don't follow."

"Lance is very bright. He understands at least fifty words, and 'bad man' are two of them. Lance would have torn him to pieces."

"Good God, Jane." She was seeing more new sides of Jane Miniter than she wanted to. She had never suspected that any of the jolly "boys" now romping in her yard had such talents.

"I asked Jill to look after Amy, but — do you suppose I could have another drink?"

"Of course. If you promise to go straight home and not breathe on Philip Marlowe if he stops you." She got up to mix herself another bloody mary. She paused at the window facing the yard for a moment. The boys were playing some game with a stick. Lance, who looked like a black-and-tan version of Pluto, currently had possession and was leading the others a merry chase.

"You were going to tell me about Howie — about Dr. Ashcroft, I mean."

"Oh, you know him?" Jane averted her eyes. "I guess I acted foolishly.

It's just that when our nonesuch thought that he'd cracked the case and was about to slap the cuffs on Amy, I pointed out that the . . . the body had probably floated down the brook to our property. I didn't actually *accuse* Dr. Ashcroft, I just pointed out that there was a commune of Devil-worshippers living a mile or so upstream."

"There's also a highway bridge upstream from your house, where anyone from Bridgeport or Boston or, God knows, Kansas City could have thrown it from a car. The stream begins here, for that matter, right outside our window."

"I know, I know! But don't you find it . . . suggestive that the stream flows by Dr. Ashcroft's place?"

"No, I don't. He wrote a couple of books on Satanism. He lives in — well, I can't even call it a commune, I think it's some kind of a study center. And he was written up in one of those grocery-store tabloids as a wizard who practices the Black Mass. I'm sorry, Jane, but none of those is a compelling reason to burn him at the stake."

Jane looked miserable. "You have to understand, Rose, I had to say *something.*"

"So did the girls who testified at the Salem witch trials. God, I'm sorry! I'm starting to sound like a self-righteous prig. It's just that I thought you — I didn't think you were the kind of person to say, 'He's different, let's throw rocks at him.'"

She saw that she'd pushed her friend to the brink of tears again. She went forward and put her arm around Jane's broad, tweedy shoulders. It was an uncharacteristic gesture, and it made her realize that she must be getting a little tight.

"You've had an awful shock. I don't know what I would have said or done in those circumstances. I probably would have accused everyone in the phone-book if I thought my son were under suspicion. I really want you and Amy to come to the party, if only to prove to yourself that Howie doesn't eat babies."

"Maybe I will. I don't suppose Marlowe would tell Howie that I was the one who brought his name up."

"God, don't call him Howie! That's one of the silly names Frank calls people. Like Rupert the Rotten Writer."

Jane threw back her head and bellowed with laughter. "That's wonderful! What does he —"

Anticipating the question, Rose deftly cut it off: "You see, Frank did the cover for one of Howie's — God *damn* it, for one of Dr. Ashcroft's books. He insisted on approving the design — he was afraid Frank would commit some inadvertent sacrilege, or whatever it's called when you insult the Devil, and that's how they know each other. I've never met him, myself."

"I guess I am curious to meet him. As a longtime student of the Wiccan religion, I'd surely love to give that silly man an earful about what a *witch* really is."

"Then that's settled. And you will bring Amy, right?"

"All right, but I'm warning you, she'll sit in a corner and glower at everyone. I'd better get back to her. I didn't realize —"

"Oh, stay and have another drink. You probably need a few after —"

"I think it's the last thing I need, honestly. I'll barely be able to drive home as it is." She stood up abruptly and — perhaps nettled by Rose's lecture — added: "I think you've had enough, too. You look as if you could use some rest."

"Methought I heard a voice cry, 'Sleep no more, Macbeth hath murdered sleep,'" Rose declaimed as they walked to the front door. She observed that Jane's step was as firm as ever, while her own was slightly less than steady. "Did you know there's a theatrical superstition that you must never, ever quote *Macbeth*? Otherwise, something horrible will happen. Hello, boys!" she cried as they stepped outside and the pack boiled around them. "You're Fang, right — no, Lance, that's it, hello, Lance. Hi, Dougall! Turn, hell-hound, turn, and let the angel whom thou still hast served tell thee, Macduff was from his mother's womb untimely *rrripped!*"

"I see you don't believe in theatrical superstitions," Jane said dryly.

Rose's high spirits abruptly collapsed. "Something horrible has already happened, I guess. Amy will get over it. She seems like a sensible girl."

"*Stolid* is the word. Anyway, you've cheered me up. For this relief, much thanks. You all here, boys? Where's Marcel? Okay, good. Bye-bye, Rose."

One of these days, Rose reflected as she waved after the retreating Bronco, she would have to learn the names of those damned dogs. Jane Miniter might get a chuckle out of "Mrs. Minotaur," but would be wounded if she kept confusing Bozo with Dougall. Marcel was not the poodle she had pictured, but a German shepherd.

The bulk of the house looming above her was suddenly oppressive. It had been designed as an industrial building, after all, not a house, and their own boxy additions had done nothing to make it homey. She sometimes imagined the caustic comments her miller-ancestor might have made upon learning that his great-great-granddaughter would one day set up housekeeping in his austere workshop.

Rupert Spencer's father, George, the lawyer who had steered her inheritance through probate and later dealt with the legal complications of converting the mill, had told her that the miller's actual home had once stood on the other side of the pond. It had burned down around the time of the Mexican War, and the miller with it. Now not even a cellar-hole marked its site.

Although George dabbled in local history, he had been able to tell her little about her ancestor beyond his name, a fanciful one for a man of his time and station: Mordred Glendower. He had probably brought the name from Wales. George had told her — hesitantly, with some embarrassment, as befitted a cautious lawyer relating gossip — that the miller had an unsavory reputation. As late as the early 1900's, the children of Mt. Tabor were warned that Mordred would get them if they didn't eat their spinach.

The miller's son had changed the family name to Glenn, which could be seen either as confirmation of the legend or an innocent effort at Americanization. For whatever reason, he had left Mt. Tabor to become an itinerant merchant. He had followed the forty-niners to California, not to search for gold, but, far more appropriately for a hard-headed Yankee trader, to sell overpriced picks and shovels to the prospectors. He had wound up owning large chunks of San Francisco and a piece of the Central Pacific Railroad.

Even though his descendants had shown tendencies toward alcoholism or insanity or both, none of them had quite managed to dissipate the family fortune. Along with the less desirable family traits, Rose's father had inherited some of the shovel-merchant's business savvy. He consolidated the family holdings into a chain of hardware stores, running them successfully for many years before selling out to a larger corporation.

Maybe the burden of inactivity had been too much for him; or maybe he had been planning his next move for years, cleverly disguising his delusions behind a sensible and businesslike mask. However it came about, he next announced his true identity as God and went off to a mountaintop retreat to grow a long white beard and enlighten his disciples, most of whom were teen-aged girls.

Rose's sister and two brothers had joined in a suit to have the old man declared insane. He was sane enough to hire a gang of cutthroat lawyers who raised a barrage of constitutional issues, most of them boiling down to one basic contention: maybe he really was God. That point became moot upon his death.

A grotesque farce then ensued, with Rose's brother Owen rushing to the mountaintop with sheriff's deputies in the nick of time to keep the disciples from disposing of the body and subsequently maintaining that the old man had been assumed physically into heaven. Without a body, the estate would have remained untouchable for years; and Owen had recently been advised by a couple of swarthy men in white-on-white shirts and pointy shoes that his Vegas markers, allowed to pile up on the strength of his great expectations, were long overdue. Cracking the will and fighting the claims of the disciples and their offspring took two years: not fast enough for Owen's creditors, who put him in a wheelchair for the rest of his life.

Rose herself had taken no part in the litigation. The baby of the family, the old man's darling, she had respected his right to do whatever he damn pleased, however crazy it might seem or inconvenient to others it might be.

He had written to her regularly and at great length. Up to a point, his letters where sensible and interesting and witty. Beyond that point, he tended to rant. He kept urging her to join him on his mountaintop, where he would teach her how to hurl thunderbolts at the blacks and the Jews and the IRS and show her how to project her astral body to eavesdrop on the innermost cabals of the Kremlin, the Vatican and the Trilateral Commission. She would agonize for hours over her measured replies, trying to humor him without encouraging his delusions. Once, she had relented and visited him; she tried hard never to think about that visit.

His will left half his fortune to her, the other half to his followers, but she didn't contest the family's efforts to discredit it. Even before his final madness, he had taken pains to regain title to his ancestor's property in Mt. Tabor, and she was delighted to settle for the mill, which nobody else wanted, and a few thousand dollars.

The mill had seemed — in Frank's words, which still made her wince — a Godsend. Despite Frank's respectable income, there was no way they could have afforded a house in the country with room for the vast studio he had always craved: certainly not a house that was so picturesque, so convenient to the city, with substantial acreage that included a pond and a stream and a small forest.

Beyond those attractions, Rose had felt an almost mystical attraction to the place. An uprooted stranger in New York, she knew that at last, at long last, she was going home: to a home even older than California, to her ancestral seat, to the demesne of Mordred Glendower, whose name sang of King Arthur and Shakespeare, chivalry and wizardry, a forgotten hero who, like her father, had been mocked and reviled by the small-minded and meddlesome.

The anticipation had been exhilarating, the homecoming had been thrilling, the first days had been idyllic. Then the dreams came: the dreams in which her Father, crowned with lightning and robed in thunder, told her that all these things had come to pass in accordance with His plan; and that her true inheritance, the seal and scepter of God's only begotten daughter, lay buried in the cellar of the mill.

Chapter Four

*T*he night of the Hallowe'en party was bearing down on him like a locomotive, and Patrick still hadn't found the courage to invite Shana. He had been alarmed when his mother suggested that he invite some friends to the party. She had never made such a suggestion before. "He couldn't figure out why she should do so now. In the past, he had been comfortable with the freedom to mingle with his parents' guests or go to his room and ignore them. This party would not give him that choice. He would be thrust into the invidious position of subordinate host, welcoming all the dorks and dweebs and airheads that he saw far too much of in school. He would be obliged to see that his guests were enjoying themselves, when his truest wish would be to weight them all down and shove them into the pond.

Except for Shana, of course, but she wouldn't come. It would be idiotic to suppose that she would. What girl would want to go to an adults' party, especially to a party where the adults would be making fools of themselves in silly costumes? Certainly no girl whom he had never taken anywhere else, not to a movie or a dance or even for a walk, certainly not a popular girl like Shana. Her inevitable refusal would end the vague and formless hope he could otherwise have continued to entertain indefinitely. She might be so offended by the invitation that she wouldn't play with him in study hall anymore. The innocent game of footsie had so escalated that he had to bring a spare pair of jeans and underpants to school in his backpack every day.

In the meantime, he didn't ask anyone else. The obstacle of asking Shana loomed like a mountain in his path. If he ever succeeded in scaling it, everything else would fall into place, but all he could do, for days on end, was stare at the mountain and despair.

Making things worse, Rose began badgering him as the time approached. Had he asked anyone? Whom would he ask? Was there a special girl he might invite? He mumbled Shana's name, and Rose threw him into a panic by suggesting that it might be easier if she were to call and invite her. He could never have lived that down. Only by promising to ask Shana himself, the very next day — no, he wouldn't call her now, he had never called her before, and telephones made him nervous — could he forestall Rose's interference.

It was fortunate that he had no bad dreams that night, since he felt ill enough the next morning, ill with terror. Only the worse fear that his mother might take it upon herself to make that damned phone call kept him from staying in bed.

He had made a point of doing his algebra homework twice, once for himself with a couple of mistakes, once for Shana with no errors. She dazzled him with one of her special smiles when he passed it to her. She swatted his hand when he tried to move hers to his crotch, but that was often her way. He stared at her as she copied, head bent, lips compressed in concentration. He followed the curve of her shell-pink cheek, half hidden by her blond hair, to the delicate hollow of her throat. His imagination took him below the triangle of skin exposed by her collar. Her breasts would fit neatly into his cupped hands. She caught him staring at her, and his cheeks burned when she flashed him another quick smile before returning to work. When he put his hand on her thigh, she shoved it aside.

The red-haired woman had coarsened him and debauched him and made him unworthy of a sweet girl like Shana. But the red-haired woman was nothing but the incarnate depravity of his own mind. He had been unworthy to start with.

He couldn't whisper an invitation to the party. He couldn't entrust such an important message to a note. He had to ask her face-to-face and accept the full measure of rejection that he would see in her eyes. When she had finished with his work and passed it back, he pretended to be absorbed in one of his books, although every nerve in his body was stretched tight and screaming with anticipation for the sound of the bell.

It rang. He leaped to his feet and whirled toward her, terrified that she might slip out or attach herself to one of her friends before he could speak.

But she spoke first. "Thanks, Patrick, you're really great to let me copy your homework like this. If I can ever pay back the favor —"

"You can. I mean, there's been something I've been meaning to ask you. We're having like a Hallowe'en party at my place on Saturday, my parents are, you know, with like costumes and all. And she said — I mean, I thought it would be a good idea to invite some of my friends, you know?"

"Like who?"

"Who?"

"Who's invited?"

"Oh. Well. You're the first, really, I haven't thought of anyone else. Some of my parents' friends are bringing kids around our own age. Like

Amy Miniter."

He wished he had a knife; he would have cut his own throat on the spot. Amy was the only person he could think of, but blurting her name out like that underlined his status as an outcast. She was a plain, awkward girl, even less socially acceptable than he was.

Shana threw back her head and shrieked with laughter. "Amy Miniter? In a Hallowe'en costume? Far fucking out! I got to see this, no kidding."

"Well, she's not the only one, I don't know, maybe some of your friends would come, too, and there's Walt Kraft —" Patrick wondered why he hadn't thought of him first, Bill and Karla's son, who was neither a misfit nor a joke, like Amy — "and some other people I'll ask. I figured that asking you first was the most important thing. So that's what I wanted to ask you, will you come? To the party? Saturday night?"

"That's what I already said, dummy. Do I have to mail you a formal acceptance?"

"You did? You will? Jesus! Terrific! That's wonderful. Great!"

"Call me about it, will you? I got to run." She left him too shocked to be ecstatic.

After school, Patrick passed up the bus and ran most of the way home. He urgently needed to burn up the energy and high spirits that threatened to make him explode at any moment. He had been wrong. There was nothing at all the matter with his appearance or his personality. Shana Jennings was his. All he had needed to do was ask. It was so ridiculously simple, it was so obvious, it had been so easy. He had been cowering under a mountain for a week and now, after one leap, he stood on top of it.

Not even the sight of the mill could dampen his mood, as it often did. It wasn't that the aspect of the place was depressing. On some summer days, from some angles — those angles from which his parents's goofy additions didn't show — it was as pretty as a postcard. Even now, surrounded by skeletal trees and sere grass, overhung by a gray sky, its appearance was one of stately but comfortable solidity. No matter what it looked like, though, it evoked half-remembered associations from all of his bad dreams. It sometimes seemed to him as if the mill stood simultaneously in two worlds, one of them invisible and intangible but just as real as the world of sight and touch.

He was bursting with his news when he entered. He was eager to tell his mother. He wouldn't blurt it out, of course, he would drop it casually into the conversation and leave it to her to point out its importance. Obviously, she was impatient with his shyness, his lack of social skills. Well, she'd been wrong, and perhaps an apology, perhaps even some praise, might be forthcoming.

She wasn't downstairs. She had probably gone off with one of her friends, as she so often did. The friend might stick around when she returned, and he didn't want to share his news with Carla Kraft or Mrs.

Miniter. It was Rose alone he wanted to impress.

But he had to tell somebody. The need to share his triumph was almost physical in its intensity. There was Frank, of course. He would be working now. Patrick had never disturbed him at work, not since he'd been a small child. Frank had never told him not to do it. It was simply something he never did. In fact he had entered his father's present studio only once, when the carpenters had still been working to convert the mill. He hadn't seen it since they'd moved in. If he needed an excuse to intrude, that would serve well enough.

He mounted the two open flights of stairs and knocked at the door.

"Yeah, come in."

Frank slumped on a stool before his easel with a can of beer in his hand. He wore his silly working costume, with the bill reversed on his Mets cap. Dressed like that, he suggested some character from an *Our Gang* comedy who had run afoul of a witch and been aged forty years overnight. His glum look fit that scenario.

"You all right?" Patrick asked.

"No. That goddamn party is hanging over us like an avalanche, and your mother is freaking out. Serves her right, it was her idea. Plus I need to find a model, and they are always a pain in the ass."

"About the party —"

"I keep drawing the same damned broad. It was fine when I was doing the last job, but now that's over, and I'm still stuck with the same face. It's ridiculous. I just can't seem to work from photographs anymore. But getting a model to come up here, assuming I could. . . . Christ, I didn't even think of that when we moved out to the sticks. I don't suppose you know any halfway decent-looking girls, do you?"

"Well, yes." Patrick tried hard not to sound smug. "I just invited one to the party."

"You did? Well, that's good, I'm glad to hear it. I mean, she's better-looking than Miss Minotaur?"

"No kidding, Frank, she's the prettiest girl in my class. She's very popular. I didn't think for a minute that she'd go, and it took me a week to find the guts for it, but I asked her today, and she said yes."

"Well, that's great. I'm really glad to hear that. See? It's no big deal. Believe it or not, deep down inside, most girls your age feel as shy and insecure as you do, even the pretty ones. Especially them, in some ways. They're just human beings, slobs like all the rest of us."

Patrick had heard all that before. While Frank talked, he wandered restlessly around the huge room, picking up sketches at random. Most of them embodied Frank's ideas for the party decorations in the Great Hall and the other ground-floor rooms. Some radiated such menace that Patrick wondered if his father could glimpse the other world in which the mill also stood, the world of his nightmares. Grouped around the studio were some papier-mâché figures that Frank had been working on for the party. Most of them had been conceived in a comical spirit, but one of them, a noseless, lidless face suggesting an imperfectly decayed corpse, topping an emaciated figure in black, didn't seem at all comical. Patrick tried to keep his eyes averted from that one. He tried to stay focused on the pleasant atmosphere of the airy studio, where the smell of paint and turpentine evoked reassuring memories.

Frank was still talking: "Although they're all the same with a bag over their heads, to paraphrase Ben Franklin. The only difference with the pretty ones, they're usually more trouble than they're worth."

"Rose is pretty."

"She is indeed. And that, if you'll pardon my saying so, is just the kind of crap that women love to pull. You make a general statement, and they immediately drag it down to the particular, usually to club you over the head with it. I wasn't talking about your mother, I was stating a general truth. And as you know, all generalities are false. What's her name?"

"The girl I invited? Shana Jennings. She's a cheerleader."

"Well, that's nice. I used to go for majorettes, myself. I think I was a pervert even then: it was the boots. Not that I ever got anywhere with them. But I guess I shouldn't ask her to pose. She might get the wrong idea, even though it's the sort of job where she can keep her clothes on."

Patrick was thrilled by a plan that might bring Shana to their house every day. He said, "She might like the idea."

"Yeah, well, I'll take a look at her. Get me a beer?"

Frank had made himself a second home up here. There was a refrigerator, an enclosed lavatory, a large couch, a hotplate, a radio and a television set. As a child, Patrick had once been surprised to see his father working on an illustration and watching television at the same time.

After handing him the beer, Patrick turned and found himself confronting a sketch on the easel.

"Who is she?" he demanded.

"That's the broad I was telling you about, the one who's screwing up my work. Everybody comes out looking like her, no matter what I do."

"But you said a photograph — ?"

"No, I said I tried to draw from photographs, but she just came out of my head. It's a shame I'm not drawing *Vampirella*. Although she was more well-rounded, now that I think of it. This looks like one of those heroin-chic models in need of a fix. Her goddamn feet are too big, don't you think? But maybe that's because I made her legs too skinny. This is the kind of stuff I shouldn't even have to think about, but she has a way of. . . . What's the matter?"

"Nothing. She looks familiar."

"Oh? Do you suppose she's somebody we know? That would explain it, although I'm sure I wouldn't forget meeting somebody like her."

Patrick had half-expected to find the red-haired woman sometime in the waking world, but never like this, in a drawing of his father's. There were discrepancies, but they could be ascribed to artistic license. Her hair was moderately curly, for instance, not straight. But he could not doubt that Frank's model lived in his dreams.

He faced an impossibility. He was looking through a rip in the fabric of the sane universe, and yet he felt neither awe nor wonder nor fear. He felt an acute pang of jealousy, and he knew he was tottering on the brink of rage. He didn't trust himself to speak as he walked from the room.

"Come again sometime," Frank called, oblivious to his son's agitation.

Patrick forced himself to be calm as he paced the rooms on the ground floor. His first reaction had been irrational, and he told himself that it would be more appropriate to feel intense relief and even gratitude toward his father. The sketch proved — well, not that he was perfectly sane, but at least that he wasn't as crazy as he had suspected. The woman was real. She had somehow made a profound impression on both of them. But she couldn't be someone they had met casually, some girl they had both noticed behind the counter at Wal-Mart. As Frank said, he wouldn't have forgotten meeting her.

Was it possible that, as a practical joke or crackpot experiment, some-one had hypnotized them, introduced them to the woman, and then erased the incident from their conscious memories? From what he had read of hypnotism, he supposed it was possible, but he couldn't imagine who would pull such an elaborate hoax, nor could he even begin to imagine the prankster's motive. Could the woman be communicating with them both by telepathy? Whether that was possible or not, he didn't know, but the hypothesis eliminated the need for a motive. She might be sending the signals unknowingly in her own dreams.

He laughed aloud as he imagined what Frank or Rose would say to either of those theories, even if he advanced them with the most elaborate qualifications and disclaimers.

But he had to talk to somebody. He had proof, in Frank's sketch, that something unnatural was going on. Bill Kraft would be at the party. As a psychologist, he might be able to explain everything — although Patrick was reluctant to open up his dreams to somebody who would know more about them than he did. Rupert Spencer would be there, too. He was intelligent and well-read, and he was an adult who talked to Patrick as a perfect equal. It would be easy to tell him. but it was questionable whether he would know what it all meant. Whomever he chose, the party would be ideal for making his choice and introducing the topic in a casual way.

He felt a twinge of annoyance with Shana. She would monopolize his time, she would drain all-important issues from his mind. He would be obliged to amuse her. He wouldn't get the chance to talk to anyone else. The invitation, the acceptance, his happiness: these things now seemed so childish that he winced. He had important things to do at the party, and he had crippled himself by hanging a pretty albatross around his neck.

Pacing through the kitchen on his restless rounds, he noticed that the cellar door stood open. He stopped and stared at it for a moment, unable to account for the sense of menace that filled him. It was only a door. Doors stood either open or closed, and this one just happened to be open. Why did the sight of it make him feel like running out of the kitchen?

His irrational fear annoyed him. Even though he couldn't shake it off, he could face it. He forced himself to walk to the door. He took the knob in his hand. He wanted to slam it shut and retreat, but he thrust another test on himself. He leaned forward and peered into the gloom.

It wasn't completely dark down there. A light must have been burning in a remote corner. He snapped the switch that should have turned on a central overhead light, but nothing happened.

He leaned casually against the jamb. Affecting a nonchalant pose, he hoped it would make him feel that way, but it didn't. His heart raced, his throat dried up. Despite the dreams, he had never been afraid of the cellar before. Now he was.

Rose said she had dreamed that something was buried in the cellar. So had he. Someone, more likely: the red-haired woman. In his least plausible scenario, she was the ghost of someone who had been buried here.

"Boo!" he sneered at himself as he lunged forward down the stone stairs.

His intention was to turn off the light. That was the sensible, reasonable thing to do. Simply shutting the door and pretending to forget about it wouldn't work. He would know that a light was burning down there, an unseen memorial to his cowardice.

Not until he was halfway down the stairs did it occur to him that, having turned off the light, he would have to retrace his steps in absolute darkness. He stopped. He should go back now and get a flashlight. But he didn't need one. The cellar was virtually empty. It held nothing to trip over, and he could find his way back to the stairs in the dark. He continued to the bottom.

The cellar was low and vaulted. It held niches that might have been bricked-up doorways, and a couple of pointless passages ended in solid walls. It seemed possible that the cellar could once have been as extensive as it appeared in his dreams. Why had parts of it been sealed off? A couple of disturbing answers scratched for admission to his mind with bony fingers, but he cut them off.

Far to the left lay the wall that faced the mill-pond. It was below the level of the pond, and it sweated and dripped perpetually. Of feeble wattage to start with, now caked with dust, the bare bulb illuminated only part of the glistening wall. He ordered himself to walk toward it.

He cried aloud when a pale shape moved at the corner of his vision.

"Patrick? It's only me."

"Mom." The rarely-used word came naturally. "You . . . startled me."

He laughed at his own talent for understatement. As a child, he had once poked his finger into a live light-socket. Nothing had happened to him since then that could be compared to this.

"What are you doing down here?" she asked.

"I saw the light, and. . . ."

He hadn't seen Rose naked for a long time. She seldom used to wear clothes around the house. She had disappointed him by abandoning that custom at about the same time her body became a major source of interest to him; and probably that was why. She wore nothing now but a pair of tennis-shoes, once white, now dark and soggy from the seepage on the floor. He tried hard to avoid looking below her neck, but he was painfully conscious of that area. It shamed him that he was becoming aroused.

". . . I thought I'd turn it off," he said, pretending there had been no long pause in his sentence. "Aren't you cold?"

"Not really." When she shrugged, making her breasts quiver, he had to look away entirely. "I didn't want to get my clothes wet and dirty, that's all."

"But what are you doing?"

She giggled. "You'll laugh at me."

"No, I won't."

"Promise."

"I promise I won't laugh."

"All right. I was looking for some kind of secret passage. I told you about my dream, didn't I?"

"Some of it."

"I've had it again. More than once. Whatever it is, it's buried behind this wall." She touched its wet, mouldy surface, then shuddered and wiped her hands together briskly.

"But that was just a dream." It didn't escape him that he was the last person who should make such a sensible comment.

"Come and look."

He followed. He despised himself for it, but he couldn't keep himself from staring at her buttocks as they clenched and slackened in a fascinating sequence. Viewed from the back, she appeared not much older than he was.

The announcement he had long planned came out sounding more petulant than happy: "I asked that girl to the party. She said she'd come."

"That's nice," Rose said, not even troubling to feign interest. "Look over here. You see how the pattern of the stonework is repeated, over and over again? But here the pattern becomes slightly different, and the inconsistent stones form a rectangle. Like a door."

At first he saw nothing but stones. He was about to tell her so when the pattern clicked together. The rectangular outline leaped out at him.

"I see it. Maybe it's just more recent than the original wall. A repair job."

She ignored his suggestion. "I've been poking and pushing and rapping to no effect." She squatted and ran her hand over the lower tiers of masonry in a caressing gesture. "Maybe we could knock one of the stones out with a hammer and chisel. What do you think?"

"You want to know what I think? That the pond would come rushing in and drown us."

"Really?" Looking up quickly, she caught him with his eyes on her breasts.

He made a lame effort to legitimize his interest: "You're getting goose-bumps. Why don't you come upstairs? It's not only damp and cold down here, it stinks."

"You're a regular mother hen." She stared at her hands with distaste, made do this time by wiping them on her buttocks. "I don't think it would hurt if we made a little hole, just to see."

"That would be like making a little hole in the bottom of a boat." He giggled. "To see the fish."

"Sometimes a little hole can be just what you need."

Despite her sly smile, he refused to believe that she was making a lewd innuendo. Yes, she was making some kind of joke, but he had misunderstood it grossly. He turned his back on her and walked to the hanging lightbulb. "How come you believe in dreams all of a sudden? Remember when you gave Carla that lecture about how her Tarot cards were bullshit?"

"That was different." Her eyes, in the overhead illumination, seemed disturbingly dark and deep-set. "The dreams . . . well, they're awfully real. And the door *is* here, just where I thought it would be. Perhaps I overheard something about this place as a child, something I've consciously forgotten. That's not quite the same thing as superstition."

He turned off the light. Her rationalizations seemed as specious as his own. He was about to question her further when the fear came sweeping back like the imagined flood from the pond. The darkness was absolute in this site of his own ghastly dreams, and his mother, invisible now, had seemed on the edge of transforming herself into the red-haired woman. He restrained himself from turning on the light again.

Rose broke the spell by giggling. "Where the hell are you? I can't see a bloody thing. I warn, you sir, if you try to take advantage of me —"

He gasped as they collided, and she laughed again. He put his hands out steadyingly and they rested on bare flesh that slid beneath his fingers as she turned to walk beside him. She put her arm through his. His arousal was complete, and it nauseated him, but he couldn't resist moving closer until his arm pressed her naked breast. The image of her large, dark nipples had been burned into his eyes.

"Oh, shit!" He had collided with something that just shouldn't be there. "What's this?"

"It's a table. And a couple of chairs. I don't recall having seen them before today, but I saw them when I came down. It means we're going in the right direction."

He had never seen them before, either, except in his dream: the dream in which he had dined on human flesh. Remembering that had an odd effect on him. It made his present desires seem less reprehensible. His dream-woman had said the feast was a kind of exercise to make him stronger. It had made him strong enough to slip his arm around Rose's bare hip until his fingertips rested at the very limit of tickling hair. She drew even closer to him as they went up the stairs.

Good God, was he on the verge of feeling up his own mother? Did she mean to allow this?

The spell, if such it was, broke under the impact of light, of stodgy appliances, of dirty dishes in the sink. "Naughty!" she cried, slapping his hand and slipping away.

She hadn't neglected to giggle and bat her eyelashes before fleeing the room, her bottom somehow even more enticing with its streaks of filth from the strange wall. Patrick believed that almost any other male would have given pursuit, father or not, and that this was what she had hoped for.

No, wait. *Father?* He was Rose's son. That walk through the dark cellar of their dreams, where certainly things were not as they seemed, had turned things upside-down. She had encouraged him to fondle her, she had joked about a "little hole —"

She dares to speak of a "little hole." That overused baggage, rather a vast cavern that demons have hammered out for a field wherein to frolic!

Patrick cried aloud. Everyone knew that "hearing voices" was a sure sign of mental disorder. But had he actually heard it, or was it a strange thought that had boiled up from the unknown depths of his mind?

It had certainly sounded like a voice.

Seeking some distraction from his thoughts, from his voices, from his incestuous desires, he remembered that he was supposed to call Shana to discuss the details of — their date? No, the details of his invitation. Such a task would normally have required him to spend an hour steeling his nerves, assuming he would have been able to do it at all. But now he was eager to phone her. She was like someone from another world, the real one, and he needed to make contact with that world.

A young male voice answered: "Hello?"

He was distracted by a bad smell. The telephone? No, it was his hand. Rose had wiped the foul seepage from the wall on her bottom, and he had stroked it. What lay out there? Was the pond clogged with corpses? He wanted to fling down the telephone and go to wash his hands, but he refused to give up, now that he had committed himself to the horror of making a phone-call to a girl.

Maybe this was a brother. Patrick said, "Hello, may I speak to Shana, please?"

"Who wants her?"

"Patrick Laughlin."

"*Who?*" The incredulity of the voice implied that the name would have been appropriate only for a Martian.

He repeated his name. "Let me speak to Shana, please."

"What —" There was a commotion in the background, protests, squeals, laughter. "What do you want to talk to her about? The big sale on pantyhose at Wal-Mart?"

Patrick lost his temper. "Look, whoever —"

"Hello, Pat?" It was Shana, breathless.

"Yes, hello, I'm calling about the party —"

"Oh, God, Patrick, I'm sorry, I can't come, I just can't."

Not yet in control of his anger, he demanded: "Why the hell not?"

"I beg your fucking *pardon.* I don't have to explain my —"

"I'm sorry." He interrupted her with the mildest voice he could summon. "It's just that — well, I'm disappointed, that's all."

The sound at the other end was abruptly muted, as if by a hand clapped over the receiver, but he thought he heard a shriek of laughter.

"I forgot, it's my grandmother's birthday —" muffled giggles, voices — "and I just can't get out of it, honest. I'm sorry. Really, I am."

"Some other time, perhaps, we could —"

"I don't know —" In the background, the boy's voice said something that sounded like "stupid asshole," but it was muted by the hand, and then Shana resumed: "We'll see."

"At least I am glad to have given you and your friend so much amusement."

"Don't mention it. You have fun with Amy Miniter now, hear?"

Finally irrepressible, Shana's laughter erupted as a wet sputter. The line went dead.

Chapter Five

*D*ecked out as W.C. Fields with squashed top-hat and putty nose, Frank rocked on his heels as he surveyed the buffet table in the Great Hall.

"Never in my born days have I beheld such a commendable collection of comestibles," he drawled in his creditable Fields-voice. "When the sheriff arrives to repossess our domicile, we can console ourself with the knowledge that for one night we dined like the Caesars."

"Don't get carried away with your role," Rose said. "You have all night to drink."

"Protein." He plucked a deviled egg from the table. "Protein inhibits the absorption of alcohol."

She sputtered something inaudible, threw up a hand in theatrical despair. He couldn't say whether her criticism was serious; certainly he had drunk no more than he usually did by this point in a Saturday evening, maybe even less. The preparations for the party, he decided, had frayed her nerves, and her mood was hard to read. Her costume didn't help. She was dressed as a vampire with white pancake makeup, green eye-shadow, and blood-red lipstick. With her lank black hair and faux-mouldy black dress, she looked like something that would have been better left unexhumed.

He tried to mollify her: "It really is a beautiful spread."

She just nodded in glum agreement, staring at the twenty-pound turkey, the whole ham glazed with honey and champagne, the innumerable trays of *hors d'oeuvres* inspired by color spreads in *Gourmet.* Karla and Jane had helped out, and even he himself had lent a hand when Jane grew obsessed with deveining the shrimp and thus unavailable for other duties, but Rose had done most of the work. She had always loved to cook. Now it looked as if she had lost that love.

"You really — oh, Christ, somebody's here already. I'll go let them in."

Rose returned to the kitchen, and he took the opportunity to top off his gin at the bar. He gave the room one last inspection as he sipped, pleased with his decorations. The Great Hall lent itself to a funereal mood.

The mill itself had given a touch of its own, something he couldn't quite pin down, that had unexpectedly raised his offhand efforts to the level of genius. The cheap black drapes and black tablecloths looked like rich velvet in the light of tall white candles; the cobwebs glinting among the beams of the lofty ceiling looked real. The *papier-mâché* figures that skulked in odd corners seemed ready to pounce. Maybe he had missed his calling by not opening a funhouse.

He had heard a car crunching gravel out front. Now the bell rang, and he went briskly through the living room. It looked just as good. A couple of logs like tree-trunks crackled in the fieldstone fireplace, and he suspected they would still be crackling just as merrily next week. Jack-o'-lanterns, Patrick's contribution, glowed in the front windows.

He flung open the door. Rain spattered his face. He confronted a magnificent and barely-clothed Amazon.

"My God! I don't remember inviting Raquel Welch, but you're sure as hell welcome. I'm Frank Laughlin."

"And this is Justine d'Estranges," said the Scarecrow of Oz, standing just behind her and a head beneath her, while the Amazon fondled Frank's proffered hand and tittered giddily. Despite her heroic construction, he now suspected that she was no more than sixteen. And a slow sixteen at that.

Frank wrenched his eyes away to examine the Scarecrow. As with Rose and he himself, the Scarecrow had chosen makeup rather than a mask to define his identity, and he had done a good job of it. Fortunately he hadn't perfected the job by shaving his neat, salt-and-pepper Vandyke, and that enabled Frank to recognize him.

"So glad you could come, Dr. Ashcroft!" He shook his hand while guiding his gorgeous satellite inside. Six or seven more of them infiltrated the room, all costumed as animals of malefic repute. Introductions of the various goats and toads and owls and wolves slipped by unnoticed as he kept his full attention on Justine.

She wore high-strapped, gold sandals, a gold tiara, and a white, transparent leotard that displayed a vast expanse of sleek, taut skin. A white bow was slung over her shoulder, a quiver of white arrows hung at her waist.

Still retaining her hand, Frank said in his Fields-voice, "I am reminded of the immortal words of Rubber Coupling, 'The uniform 'e wore wasn't very much before, And rather less than 'arf of that behind.' Who're — oops, forgive me — who *are* you supposed to be?"

"Diana, of course." It was Ashcroft who answered. "The Huntress."

"Ah." He let go of her hand. "As I recall, the last guy who saw this much of her got zapped into a stag. Am I safe?"

"Perhaps the costume isn't consistent with a goddess allegedly chaste, but Justine likes to show off her body. It's all she's got."

What seemed the cynical cruelty of the comment embarrassed Frank, but only until Justine unleashed a peal of laughter. So he said, his eyes on her, "Well, who could ask for anything more?" and that provoked further squeals. "The bar's in the next room, everyone please come along and help yourselves. My wife — ah, here's my son, Patrick."

Patrick shook hands with Dr. Ashcroft and was introduced to his menagerie. Frank was impressed with the cool way he accepted his introduction to Justine, neither leering at her near-nudity nor wincing at her brainless guffaws.

Patrick had given no thought to his costume. His parents, coping with other problems, hadn't considered it, either. The lapse was discovered only at the last minute. Frank, stealing a quip from Robert Mitchum, suggested that he show up naked, splash himself with ketchup and say he was a hamburger.

Carla Kraft came through. On the Fourth of July and any other remotely-suitable occasion, she said, George Spencer and his cronies would dress as Minutemen and get together to fire muskets and cannon, march here and there, and otherwise disport themselves patriotically. Carla made a phone call, determined that one of George's comrades shared Patrick's build, and a costume was provided. His black hair was long enough to provide a suitably ratty ponytail. He had improved on the costume with a black eyepatch.

Accompanying him in the general direction of the bar, Frank noticed that he limped. "Something wrong with your foot?"

"I don't know, it seems to go with the outfit."

"Yeah, I think it works. An eighteenth-century guy who's been through the mill."

The mill. Frank mulled that one over.

". . . but as you know," Ashcroft was saying, "Diana is a cognate of Hecate, who holds a special place in our hearts. She hunted at night with a pack of savage animals. The group has a theme."

"Except for the Scarecrow," Frank said. "Where do you fit in?"

"I stand apart." Ashcroft poured himself a stiff bourbon and reluctantly added a single icecube. "It would be inappropriate for me to wear anything that had special significance."

"So Kermit the Frog would have been okay."

"Yes, that would have been good. I just didn't happen to think of it."

"Dr. Ashcroft?"

"Ah, Mrs. Laughlin? You look very . . . *natural.*"

Rose giggled uncertainly, but Frank caught on that it was a compliment suitable for a corpse in a funeral parlor. They were urging first names on each other — not Howie, but Howard — when the bell rang again.

Mrs. Minotaur hadn't followed his script, either. No bull's head, but Robin Hood and one of his Merry Men: a pale mouse he took to be her daughter.

"Hey, there, Jane, if things get dull, you can have a bow-and-arrow fight with Diana. This must be . . . Emma?"

"Amy," the girl whispered, studying his shoes. "How do you do?"

With a greeting like that, he thought, she should get along great with Patrick. Before he could properly chide himself for that slur, the stereo hit him like a blow between the shoulders: *Sympathy for the Devil,* a good opening choice.

"It's pissing down outside, Frank, let us in." Jane bulled her way through. "Who are you supposed to be, Robert Vesco?"

"Now, now, my fuzzy little wish-wash," he started in his Fields-voice, but the Miniters were already on their way to the Great Hall and more people were arriving. It occurred to him only as he was turning to greet the new batch that she'd been making fun of him.

Rupert Spencer was a male version of Justine. They were both proportioned in the way termed "heroic" in art school, with longer legs and smaller heads than the common run of humans. He had forgotten how much he disliked Rupert.

"Hi, Rupert. Good to see you, George. And . . . Marge?"

"Madge, you dirty old man. Is Rose dressed as Mae West?"

"We tried, but we couldn't find enough padding. Come in, come in."

The three harlequins in various combinations filed past, all with domino masks. Compared to his other guests, he thought, they showed a lack of imagination.

"Was Patrick successful?" George was a trim, silver-haired man of sixty or so, for whom the adjective "fit" might have been invented. "The costume," he prodded when Frank stared blankly.

"Oh, yes, just fine. Thank you, George. He's modified it to make himself look like Simon Gerty."

"Who?"

"Wasn't that John Carradine's character, in *Drums Along the Mohawk. . . .*" Frank saw no point in continuing, now that he had ushered them through the gates of hell. The sound in the Great Hall was deafening. Rats and cats and outlaws of Sherwood, goddesses and Minutemen and corpses and scarecrows twisted and capered and writhed in the mortuary gloom to the strains of *Rip This Joint.* The only trouble with this party was that he couldn't sneak out and go home.

He watched Justine's outrageously undulating ass until the doorbell rang again. The strap of her garment had worked its way between her cheeks until there was very little indeed to be imagined. He was pleased to see her dancing with Patrick, but his pleasure was not unmixed. From now on would he drool and nod and gum his milktoast, approving his son's success with women that he himself lusted for? He trudged heavily to the front of the house.

"My God, who're you? No, don't say a word, let's get out of here, I love you!"

"Frankie, you cock-teaser!" cried the vision at the door, and Frank wished he could melt and trickle through the floorboards: she was Alfred Roberts.

He tried to laugh as if he hadn't been fooled and stepped aside to admit the group. "I hate to break this to you, Alfie, but there's another girl at the party with your outfit."

Roberts flashed him a coy smile as he slithered past. The impersonation was brilliant. If he hadn't known Roberts, he would have accepted him as a strikingly pretty girl — as in fact he had just done, he thought glumly. Even more striking was his costume, suggesting a conspiracy. Justine's garment and her quiver and bow were white; Alfred's were black. Her sandals and tiara were gold; his were silver. Otherwise their costumes were the same. He had even waxed his truly remarkable legs.

"This is Zorro." Alfred indicated a huge young man in black motorcycle jacket and ducktail haircut, mirror sunglasses and stomper boots. Frank got the feeling that the hairdo was the only effort he'd made to change his everyday appearance.

"Wait a minute, Alfred, who the hell are you supposed to be?"

"Hecate. Say hi to my troop of wild beasts."

They had followed the *motif* of Ashcroft's entourage. But whereas Ashcroft's beasts were baleful, Alfred's were a phantasmagoria of feathers and sequins and mesh stockings and spiked heels. His bat wore Elton John glasses and his goat had a pink tutu.

"I guess you know Howard Ashcroft, huh?" Frank got no answer, for they had reached the edge of pandemonium. The group was rapidly digested.

Frank realized that he hadn't had a drink since the arrival of the first guests, and he plunged toward the bar to correct that mistake. Rose and Howie were deep in conversation there. The Rolling Stones still held the floor, so he was forced to sidle quite close to eavesdrop.

". . . brought me to the area in the first place," Ashcroft said.

"Mordred did?"

". . . vibrations . . . holy center . . . great wizard. . . ."

"Hi, Frank. I'm so glad you thought to invite Howard."

"Did you notice the last bunch of guests?" he tried to ask Ashcroft, but it was obvious that he couldn't be heard.

"Howard actually tried to buy the mill."

". . . litigation. . . ."

"What are you talking about?"

"Isn't that a magnificent woman, Frank?" She gestured at Justine, who was now dancing with Ashcroft's bat.

"An *excessive* woman." He gave Rose a hug. It wasn't entirely insincere, since he hoped to make her benefit from all the feelings Justine had churned up. Maybe they could steal away for a few minutes, once the party got rolling. "What do you mean, he tried to buy the mill?"

"When it was tied up in the courts," Rose shouted. "Only the legal tangle was so hopeless that he couldn't. So he bought a place down the road."

"Oh, I see. Please excuse me."

The thick walls of the kitchen held out all but the thudding bass and some of the wilder shrieks. He heard a thin voice droning.

". . . baby. He actually thought that I was the mother of the baby, and that I'd gotten rid of it by throwing it in the brook. And that I'd burned it first and cut it up."

Frank was unprepared for such a narrative. As soon as he grasped its nature, he tried to retreat. But Patrick and Amy had seen him.

"Hi, kids. Mind if I join you?"

Amy nodded. Her eyes, seen for the first time, were as pale as her skin and hair. *Robin Hood and his Mirthless Wraiths*, he thought.

"I —" Frank cleared his throat. He had been searching for an apt comment about Amy's weird recital, but he was shocked out of it by his son's appearance. He looked even more alone and palely loitering than Amy. "Are you okay, Pat?"

"Yes, sure, it's kind of noisy and smoky out there. Do you suppose I could have a beer?"

"Yeah, in the icebox. Would you like something, Amy? A glass of wine? I know I shouldn't contribute to the delinquency of a minor, but what kind of a dirty old man would I be if I didn't?"

"I'd like a beer, too, please, Mr. Laughlin."

"Two, Patrick. It's Frank, dear. I couldn't help overhearing —"

"Who's the blond woman in the black handkerchief?" Patrick interrupted as he returned with the beers. Amy continued her descent into hell, as her mother would doubtless have seen it, by declining a glass.

"I meant to tell you about —"

"She's *awfully* pretty," Amy said.

"I guess that's the word for it. That's somebody I know from New York." He was unwilling to squelch Amy after her gush.

"I wish I could have worn something like that, something really daring, but my mother would never have heard of it."

Frank took a slug of gin and tried not to laugh as he contemplated a vision of Amy in something daring: a mouse-costume with a scandalously short tail? Oh, hell, why not something daring? She was young. She probably had a firm ass, buoyant little tits. A touch of makeup would have done wonders for the pallid blur of her face. Thinking of her that way, he decided that she would look a lot better naked than in her dopey Robin Hood suit. He didn't neglect to consider the possibility that he had reached the stage in his drinking when any female would look better naked, but he resisted it. He was cold sober.

In retrospect, this belief was undercut by his next remark. But it was merely an outburst of generosity, something he might have done sober. It was certainly no reason for wishing he had cut out his tongue before speaking. He liked Amy, and he felt sorry for her. She was pathologically shy; she had a noisy, brassy crypto-bulldyke for a mother. The worst thing that could be said about her appearance was that it was egregiously inconspicuous.

So he said: "How would you like to pose for me sometime, Amy?"

"Don't tease me, Mr. Laughlin!" Her face actually turned red.

"*Frank,* and I'm not teasing you, honey. I'm very serious. I'd pay you to pose."

"I don't look like a model!"

"If you saw Kate Moss on the street, would you think she looked like a model? And drawing you would be a lot easier than sitting alone in my studio and trying to create women out of photographs and empty air." That was true: he could no longer do that. Amy's blandness might exorcise the spirit that held his brush.

"Is he teasing me, Patrick? He's kidding, isn't he?"

Patrick stared down at the table for a moment. The tricorne hat, the black patch, the drawn, white face — he could have been a Salem judge about to announce that all defendants would now be hanged. Instead, he handed Frank the nicest compliment he had ever been paid, suggesting that his son really understood him, but coupled with a hook that made it impossible for him to weasel out.

"My father is always kidding, Amy, but he doesn't lie. He wants you to pose for him."

"Yes, yes, I'd love to!" After a pause, she added: "I'll have to ask my mother."

"*Tell* your mother. It's your life."

"Can I quote you on that?" Patrick said with a sly smile.

Frank decided it was time to leave. He remembered that he hadn't questioned her about the story she'd been telling when he entered. Since she hadn't volunteered to tell him, he thought it better not to ask.

"I mean it, Amy. Call me, we'll work out the details."

"Thank you . . . Frank."

In the Great Hall the noise had somewhat abated. Fewer people danced, perhaps because the discs had cycled to a "Hallowe'en Classics" album and *Monster Mash.* If Frank remembered correctly, *Night on Bald Mountain* would be next. Patrick had bought that stupid disc when he was twelve, but he doubted that Patrick had put it in the player.

Bats and birds and androgynes — oh my! — muttered and ruffled their fur or feathers or clicked their hoofs in dim corners. Ashcroft apparently concurred with Carlos Castenada's *brujo* in believing that every room holds a special place where one feels most thoroughly at home; and for Ashcroft, that was at the bar. Now he was holding forth to George and Madge Spencer. Frank didn't see Rupert. He didn't see Rose, either.

Across the room, the two goddesses held a lively chat. They were about the same height. Roberts was slimmer, his blond wig a little fluffier, but his legs were very nearly as good. It still rankled that he had been fooled at much closer range. He didn't like the joke. Roberts tossed back his tresses with a graceful hand. His nails had been polished black. He had shaved his armpits. The more Frank watched, the angrier he became. He decided that his most reasonable course would be to stop watching.

*H*e made his way to the bar, exchanging greetings and playing the genial host, but not letting himself get sidetracked. He didn't recognize half the new arrivals, but that was only to be expected. They knew only a few of their neighbors, and they had urged their friends to bring other friends. Patrick had supposedly asked some kids from school, too, so it would have been impossible to identify a gate-crasher. *Any gate-crasher would be preferable to that naked fairy.* Frank tried hard to wrench his mind away from that grievance. Maybe this would be a good time to sneak upstairs with Rose. Where the hell was she?

"This is a really super party, Frank," Madge said as he refilled his gin. "Like *The Masque of the Red Death.*"

All his guests seemed determined to insult him. Before his anger could boil over, he noticed that her tone and manner implied a compliment.

"I guess you mean the picturesque qualities, not the horrible ending."

"Did it have a horrible ending? I just remember a lot of weird people having a good time. And a clock. There was a funny clock in it, wasn't there? Why won't you ask a girl to dance?"

He hated to dance, and he did it poorly. "I have to find Rose, some crisis with the food or something." He knew his smile was so false that it probably came with an audible click as he said, "But save me the waltz."

He slipped into the crowd and soon found himself staring at Roberts again. He tried to convince himself that his guest's behavior wasn't an outrage, an abomination. Nobody else was staring. Most of the people were probably fooled by his masquerade, and the others just didn't care.

He made his way to the living room, where the party hadn't yet overflowed: except for Rose and Rupert, heads together in earnest conversation by the fireplace. He sang, under his breath:

Then one rainy Hallowe'en, Steve King came to call,
Saying, "Rupert you are such a jerk, will you help write my next work?"

They didn't hear him, fortunately. Their mutual absorption was so great that he hesitated to interrupt. Then he remembered that he was her husband.

"So, here you are."

"How's the party going?"

"That's a good question. As the hostess, isn't it odd that you should have to ask it?"

He knew that his words came out sounding more belligerent than he intended, but he wouldn't apologize. Before he could speak again, Rupert said: "Rose was talking about her father, and I guess I'm guilty of drawing her out. He sounds like a fascinating character."

"He was nuts." To Rose, he said: "Don't you think you should circulate —"

"My God, Frank, this isn't the Governor's Ball! Everyone's having a marvelous time. I can see that from where I am. What's the point of *circulating* when I can't even hear myself think in there?"

Her counterattack startled him. Maybe he had been unjust. He switched to another sore point: "What do you think of that cocksucker Roberts coming here with his bare ass hanging out?"

"Who?" Rupert asked, prepared to be amused.

"Frank, if bare asses offend you, why didn't you start complaining when what's-her-name showed up? What the hell is bugging you?"

"It isn't the same thing at all!"

Rupert made polite noises as he tried to get away, but he was trapped against the fireplace between them. They both ignored him.

"It is *precisely* the same thing. Unless you are trying to tell me that nudity is acceptable in inferior creatures, like dogs or cows or women, but that men —"

"That isn't a man, you stupid bitch! Don't you see that he's putting us on, insulting us in our own home? If you can't see the difference —"

"Why don't you go take a little nap, Frank? I told you not to start hitting the sauce so early."

His hand trembled with the effort of withholding a blow. Soon he was trembling all over. "God damn you," he growled, turning and stalking back to the Great Hall.

He went straight to the bar, this time making no show of geniality. He pushed people out of his way. He had downed one stiff drink and poured another before he was again in control of his temper.

"Nice party," the Scarecrow said, edging closer. "You have to come to mine."

He stared at Ashcroft, already regretting his fight with Rose, even though it had been her own damned fault: ignoring their guests to giggle in the inglenook with her protégé at the very moment when he wanted her to ignore their guests and slip upstairs with him.

The Scarecrow was waiting for an answer. "I beg your pardon?"

"I said, you'll have to come to our party."

"Your Hallowe'en party? I imagine it's rather different."

"Oh, not at all. A few extra formalities, like the Black Mass."

"Whose idea was the gag with the costumes? I wasn't aware that you and Alfred Roberts knew each other."

"We don't."

"You're telling me it's a coincidence? The two goddesses, the beasts —"

"Special places play tricks on people. This is a special place, as I told your wife. But if you insist on a pedestrian explanation, there was an obscure Off-Off-Broadway show a couple years back that suggested the costumes to me. *The Wild Hunt,* it was called, by Martin Paige. Maybe we both saw the same play."

Frank was surprised to note how much this simple explanation relieved him. Some ratty little storefront theater near Tompkins Square, that was just the sort of place for Alfie to be found. Maybe Ashcroft shared more than one of his tastes. He scanned the room. He couldn't see Roberts now, but he saw Justine, alone for once. He felt a strong urge to go keep her company.

"Is she —" Frank found it difficult to chose the right word — "your. . . ?"

"My girlfriend?" Ashcroft's snigger was singularly unpleasant. "The Huntress is everybody's girlfriend. Don't forget to use a rubber."

Frank tried hard not to show how offensive he found Ashcroft's attitude. They had invited him here, after all, for his shock value. But he couldn't resist making a thrust in return.

"I thought that jealousy was one of the Seven Deadly Sins. Won't you have to confess your lack of it?"

Ashcroft merely laughed.

"Maybe you can clear up something I've always wondered about. Sloth is another one, and yet if you really threw your heart into it, you couldn't do much of anything else. Could you lie around on your ass all the time and still be considered a proper limb of Satan?"

"That would be a good question to ask Justine."

Frank cursed his blunder in feeding him such a line, but he joined in Ashcroft's laughter with another nearly-audible click. He poured a glass of cider, Justine's apparent preference, and drifted out of Ashcroft's orbit.

He was immediately waylaid by Robin Hood. "Where's Rose hiding?"

"In the living room." He tried to edge past.

"No, she isn't. I was just out there."

He made a pretense of looking for Rose while checking to see if Justine was still alone. "Try the kitchen."

"I looked there, too. Amy is sulking out there and monopolizing Patrick's time. He's too much of a gentleman to leave her to stew in her own juices. She's become impossible lately. Just the other evening, we were supposed to go to dinner at her grandmother's house — Arnold's mother, that is, my late husband's —"

Frank felt like Little John when he'd disputed the right of way with Jane's prototype. He managed to squeeze by her, holding up the two glasses. "I'm on an errand of mercy, I'll have to hear all about it later."

He didn't wait to see her reaction as he puzzled his way through the human maze beyond the Minotaur. The music had just cranked up again, *Highway to Hell,* making his progress tricky as the pack writhed and flailed. He saw Justine approached by a tall masquerader who had subordinated good taste to realism in his impersonation of a decaying corpse. Who the hell was he? But he was gone by the time Frank next glimpsed her through the dancers. Unexpectedly, she watched his approach and smiled. She seemed to be expecting him. Maybe the corpse had warned her, "Here comes an old letch to grope your ass." It was too much to hope that she actually liked him.

"Hi, would you like to sit this one out? I brought you a drink."

She took the cider and let him guide her to a love seat in an alcove by the stairs. When they sat down, he couldn't be sure whether she was deliberately pressing close to him or if he was crowding her with his embarrassing bulk. Either way, it was pleasant.

"Are you from around here? Originally, I mean. I suppose you're at Howard's place now, but I wondered if you came from the area or from someplace else."

She shrugged, studying him with amusement. Considering her name, he began to wonder if she spoke English. Maybe she didn't, and that was why Ashcroft had felt free to speak so contemptuously of her when they'd arrived. He put his arm around her shoulders — to make them less crowded, he assured himself — but she then pressed even closer. Her garment was all but transparent, and she wore nothing under it.

"I've been thinking of hiring some models locally." He paused to clear his throat. "And you're certainly the best-looking girl I've seen around here. Do you suppose you'd be interested? See, I'm an artist, I do all sorts of things — magazines, advertising, book jackets, whatever I can get, and I tend to specialize in women. I work mostly from photographs, sometimes working with a model when I run into problems, but finding them up here isn't easy. Not problems, I mean, those are all over the place. What do you say?"

She shrugged again, staring as if in puzzlement. Her eyes were an unusual shade of grayish green, speckled with gold flecks. He suppressed the fancy that there was no mind at all behind them and he was talking to a gorgeous automaton.

"You're a regular chatterbox, aren't you?" he said nervously as she pressed closer, searching his face with her strange eyes. "I have to admit I was kind of pissed off when somebody else showed up in your outfit. I was sure you were both putting me on in some way, but Howie assured me it was all innocent, that you all got your ideas from some play. Jesus, sweetheart, you're letting me babble. Why don't you say something?"

She laughed, low and throaty. Her fingertips traced patterns on his upper thigh. At last she proved that she could speak English. Leaning forward, trailing her fingertips over his almost painful erection, she whispered, "You have got one mother of a boner. Do you want to do me?"

"Yeah, why didn't I think of that?" He half rose to scan the dance floor and assure himself that they were not observed. "Go upstairs, two flights. The door to your left, that's my studio. I'll just circulate a little bit, show the flag, and I'll join you in five minutes."

"Hurry. I need it bad."

Instead of circulating, Frank remained on the love seat, stunned. Nothing like this had ever happened to him, and he felt none of the elation he should have upon making a conquest. But in this case he was no conqueror. He was more like an innocent bystander who happened to be in the path of a tornado. Too late, he swiveled his head in the hope of catching a glimpse of her magnificent ass as she mounted the stairs.

His five minutes weren't up, but he rose and gave the party a last, guilty survey. Then he slipped up the stairs after her.

Chapter Six

*R*ose soon regretted her impulsive flight from the house. The night was black, and the path by the pond was slimed with leaves and ribbed with exposed roots. The gusting rain must be ruining her makeup, and she shivered in her flimsy dress. Nevertheless, she refused to return just yet.

Rupert had pursued her with an umbrella. She would have appreciated a coat much more. Despite his best efforts, the umbrella kept tangling in branches, exposing them fully to the rain at odd moments and occasionally drenching them with a flood jarred free from a spruce bough. He kept up a muttered stream of curses at the path and the trees and the rain, but he didn't damn her obstinacy.

She stopped, hoping to avoid further soaking. He tripped and stumbled against her, simultaneously cursing and apologizing. She hugged herself against the cold as the rain came down harder. It hissed on the pond like steam and rattled like pebbles in the leaves around them.

"You ought to go back." There was tremor in his voice. "It's cold and wet out here."

"I've noticed. But I feel like staying for a while. There's no point in your staying with me."

"I'll stay." He was silent for a moment, and then he blurted: "Rose, I don't see why an intelligent and sensitive woman like you, why any woman, puts up with the sort —"

"Oh, cut it out, Rupert!"

"No, I won't cut it out!" He gripped her arm, a gesture more impatient than affectionate. "He milks that temperamental artist routine for all it's worth, constantly putting you down and making you fetch and carry like a slave. Why do you stand for it?"

"He's just a little drunk, that's all."

"I'm not just talking about tonight. I'm talking about every time I've ever seen him. He never lets you finish a sentence, he tells you to shut up if he doesn't like what you're saying, he orders you to get this and get that like a spoiled child."

"He only acts that way because you're around, Rupert. He doesn't like you."

"I'm sure he doesn't like any of your friends, anyone who distracts you from worshipping at his throne. Don't you ever feel that there's something more for you in life than being a doormat? Don't you ever want to use that wonderful mind of yours for anything except making shopping lists?"

"We've been through this —"

He shocked her by jerking her forward and kissing her. Out of curiosity she let him kiss her for a while, then twisted her face away.   .

"I love you, Rose."

"Oh, Rupert, I suppose I love you, too, in a way. But I love my husband."

She pushed at his chest, somewhat disappointed when he stepped back without resisting.

"This isn't the place to talk about it," he said.

"No place is. Please, Rupert, let's go inside now and forget about it."

He put his arm around her shoulders as they walked back toward the mill. He shivered, too. Maybe this episode would bring him to his senses. His attentions were becoming embarrassing. Unfortunately, they were also a bit thrilling. She tried to squelch the thrill by recalling that he was a not-too-talented writer who still lived with his parents. His arm was so strong and firm around her shoulders because he had plenty of time to work out at the gym in the mall. Did he hope to sweep her away from all this to a room in his father's house, where he would push aside his old model airplanes and cover up his *Penthouse* posters? But she hoped he wouldn't come entirely to his senses.

"Rupert —"

"What is it?"

"I just remembered something I've been meaning to ask you. But this is no time to ask you a favor. I'm sorry. Just forget it."

"Anything. I hope you're going to ask me to murder your husband." She giggled. "It was just . . . silly."

"What is it?"

"I wanted you to help me knock a hole in the wall of the cellar."

His step faltered. "Why?"

"I . . . there was a family tradition, a legend about a sort of buried treasure. I think I've found the place."

"Won't Frank do it?"

"He isn't very handy with tools, and he tends to put things off. I haven't even bothered to tell him. It's just a sort of whim, that's all. I thought it might be fun. A shared adventure."

He was silent for a while as they picked their way toward the bright lights of the mill. She found it hard to conceal her vexation. She thought that her timing and approach had been perfect.

"Well?" she asked. "What's the matter?"

"As you said, Rose, Frank doesn't like me. I don't think he'll like me any better if I go knocking holes in his walls without telling him. I'm just not the man for the job. What about Patrick?"

"I thought the idea would appeal to you. I see that it doesn't."

"If Frank approves —"

"You didn't ask his permission when you kissed me."

"That's not fair! You know —"

"I suppose it isn't. I'm sorry. I'm being unreasonable, as Frank so often tells me." They had reached the rear of the house, and she moved quickly to the kitchen door. "Forget it, Rupert, it's unimportant."

"No, I —" he started to say, but she left him behind, fumbling with the open umbrella, while she hurried through the kitchen to an adjacent bathroom and locked herself in.

She hoped she hadn't overplayed her hand. Infatuated though he might be, Rupert wasn't stupid. His reasons for refusing were sensible. Since Patrick wouldn't help her and Frank was hopeless, she would have to do it herself.

She touched up her ghoulish makeup, which had survived better than she'd thought, and returned to the kitchen. Amy Miniter, whom she typically hadn't noticed on her way in, sat alone at the table with an untouched ham sandwich and a bottle of beer.

"Why aren't you out front having fun, Amy?"

"I was. I just got hungry, that's all."

She suspected that the girl had spent the evening here, but she saw no point in trying to force her to enjoy herself. She had always sensed a sullen insolence underlying Amy's mousy demeanor.

"Maybe Patrick's other friends have arrived. Why don't you come and see when you've finished?"

"Sure." Amy bit off a mouthful of the sandwich to end the conversation.

The front door bell had rung during their exchange, and now it was ringing again more insistently. She supposed that no one else could hear it over the music. Good Lord, who had dug that old record out? The Dead Kennedys singing *Too Drunk to Fuck*. Maybe no one had noticed it, and turning it off would only draw attention, so she hurried through the Great Hall. The crowd had swelled in her absence, and so had the noise. Perhaps she should have made her invitations more specific. She wondered if there would be enough food and drink for this mob.

She reached the door at the same time as Patrick. He was still affecting a limp, and even his normal expression had subtly changed as if to suit his costume. He looked oddly older. Perhaps he possessed a hidden talent as an actor. Developing it might be a way of curing his shyness.

"Have your friends arrived yet?"

"No, I don't think so. I'm not sure." He opened the door to cut off her questions.

"Paddy, me bhoyo!" Bill Kraft cried. "We were afraid that the cock crew, and that you'd all gone back to your graves. Rose, you are a sight to beguile a necrophile."

Bill advanced to give her a hug and attempt a kiss made difficult by his yellow fangs of wax. He wore an orange fright-wig and a lab coat. She wasn't sure what he was supposed to be until his son Walt clumped in as Frankenstein's monster, followed by Carla as the Bride in lightning-streaked wig and floor-length nightgown. This outfit was less modest than Justine's, now that it had been rained on, and Rose was somewhat taken aback to realize that her friend and contemporary was centerfold material. She would have to remember to steer her away from Frank, who must be loaded out of his mind by now.

"You're all wet," Bill said, and she supposed she was giving everyone an eyeful, too; a much more limited eyeful.

"The churchyard . . . is always . . . damp," Rose groaned, gliding back from his embrace.

"Captain Kidd?" Carla was asking Patrick, gazing into his unpatched eye. "Oh, I know! Cotton Mather."

"Damme, Goodwife Kraft, 'twas yourself got me the loan of this newfangle raiment, look you," Patrick answered in an odd voice.

"What the hell have you people been smoking?" Bill asked. "And where can I get some? Your average teen-age clown can do an Irish brogue, but it remains for Patrick to do a bang-on Welsh accent. With colonial overtones, no less."

"The curse of erudition," Patrick said in the same voice.

"Love it! You're nuts. But I mean that as a compliment. Most of the people I have to deal with are merely neurotic."

"Right this way, if you want to deal with some more of them." Patrick gestured toward the Hall.

"Any decent chicks, Pat?" Walt asked him as he lumbered by.

"Try the kitchen."

"I heard that," Rose whispered. "That was cruel."

"To whom?" Patrick asked with an unpleasant smile. When he saw she had no ready answer, he said, "I've been trying to keep Amy amused all evening, because I feel sorry for her, but she doesn't want to be amused. Let Walt have a try. Have you seen Justine?"

"Who?"

"The girl Dr. Ashcroft brought."

"I . . . ah . . . no, I haven't." She resisted her first impulse to tell him that Justine was the last thing he needed. She was about his age, despite her apparent maturity. Any criticism she might offer would be based on prudery and snobbery, two voices she had always detested. It was nevertheless hard to stick to her principles when her only son wanted to stroll blithely into the man-eating jaws of a brazen slut. The least she could do was ask pointedly, "Where are your friends?"

"I don't think they're coming." He eased away from her.

"But you said — you told me you asked a girl. What happened? Do you suppose she needs a ride? I could —"

"You weren't much interested when I told you she was coming, so I figured you'd be less interested when she changed her mind." He had succeeded in edging beyond the range of normal conversation, and now he turned and slipped away.

She gestured despairingly at the empty air and went to dump herself in a secluded wing chair near the door. She would have liked to be closer to the fire, but refugees from the Hall were milling around it. She didn't feel at all sociable.

What a lovely party! She'd had a fight with Frank, the bitterest in some time, over absolutely nothing. By trying to manipulate Rupert so clumsily, she had probably lost her — her what? He wasn't her lover. *Admirer,* without the dirty little leer that Frank brought to the word, was probably accurate. And if Patrick succeeded in his current mission, he'd probably catch syphilis, if he was lucky, or AIDS, thus putting the finishing touch on another merry revel at the madcap Laughlins'.

It was all Frank's fault. If she had been permitted to continue raising Patrick the way she'd started, the way a child should be raised, without the crippling handicaps of sexual repression, he wouldn't be afraid of normal, healthy girls. He wouldn't be impelled to chase after naked whores like Justine d'Estranges simply because the sight of a female body overwhelmed his judgment. She could still work up a rage by recalling how Frank had thwarted her plans for her son's upbringing. In his crude, evil-minded phrase, he had accused her of teaching Patrick to *feel her up* for her own gratification. *Incestuous cockteaser* was only one of the ugly names he'd hurled at her. It would have been far more vile, far more truly *sinful,* if she'd slapped his hands away when he tried to explore the unfamiliar parts of her body.

She and Patrick had been reading together — Wallace Stevens, she unexpectedly recalled — alternating stanzas aloud and discussing their meaning. In *Sunday Morning,* of course, Stevens had meant that you should forget all that God-nonsense and enjoy the pleasures of the flesh, but their contact had been perfectly innocent, perfectly natural.

And then Frank had stormed in like the butt of a French farce, indignant, sputtering, turning red — easily done after a three-martini lunch with an art director or perhaps a pint of gin shared in some model's bed. When Patrick had been sent from the room, no doubt carrying a burden of guilt that he would never overcome or even understand, Frank had ordered her never again to *flaunt* her naked body to her son.

She had obeyed for several reasons: chiefly, because she had fallen into the lazy habit of doing whatever he said to avoid unpleasantness. She'd done it for Patrick's sake, too. Nothing could have been worse for his normal development than re-runs of Frank's horror-show. And the last reason was her own suspicion — foolish, of course, complete nonsense, but it gnawed at the edge of her brain — that her own motives weren't entirely pure, that Frank had hit upon a nasty truth to which she herself was blind. After all, it *had* felt good, but that was entirely beside the point. Gratifying a student's eager curiosity should make any teacher feel good.

In one sense, her motives couldn't have been pure, because the source of her desire to raise Patrick in a sexually free environment had been tainted by her own, unnatural childhood. That was a foolish argument. By the same sort of reasoning, all psychiatrists are drawn to their profession because they're crazy. But whatever its objective merits, it reinforced her suspicion; and if Frank had known about it — but that was unthinkable. The bastard would never have let her live it down.

Except legally, the sterile province of the Torquemadas and the Cotton Mathers, she couldn't call it rape. She had cooperated, perhaps she had even led him on, but she'd been only twelve years old when her father had first crept into her bed. The experience had scared her and shamed her, but — to use the phrase she'd used at the time — it had been *kind of fun.* Now she shared a weird secret with her father, and that had been a large part of the fun. Since she loved her father intensely, since she believed he was nearly perfect, she knew that she must be at fault for feeling scared and ashamed. She fought against those feelings, but she never really overcame them.

Even more bookish and withdrawn than Patrick, and certainly more dedicated to her schoolwork, she had been accepted by Swarthmore when she was only fifteen. While she was away at school the next year, her father's religious delusions blossomed. She blamed herself.

Meanwhile she read everything she could lay her hands on about sexual customs and disorders and taboos. The ancient Egyptians, who had married their fathers and mothers and sisters and brothers whenever the whim struck them, would have fallen down laughing at her pangs of guilt. So would those Polynesians who made a point of sleeping with their normally taboo relatives on special holidays. If she felt guilty, it was only because she was a narrow-minded, twentieth-century American.

Nothing that she read touched off such an explosion in her consciousness as the works of Wilhelm Reich. Not only was the man right in calling for total sexual liberation, he spoke the very thoughts that had long churned unspoken in her own mind. Of course he had been hounded and vilified by the government, of course his books had been burned at the stake, he was just like her! She underwent Reichian therapy for a couple of years, becoming the subject of frequent complaints when she would try to scream her way out of her anxieties and frustrations in the locked bathroom of her college dorm.

Finally she grew disenchanted. Reich was just another organized system of ignorance, like astrology or communism. But even after she had given up on screaming-rooms and cloudbusters and orgone-boxes, she clung to the ideas that had drawn her to Reich in the first place, the teachings that demolished repression. She determined that her children, if she ever had any, would be free from such soul-destroying bondage.

When at last she was twenty, a graduate student, a poised young woman with her own ideas and ambitions and fully-developed character, she felt strong enough to confront her crazy father on his mountaintop. She knew that she would no longer feel guilt or fear in his presence, but she was totally unprepared for what she did feel: intense, physical desire. She came to her senses and fled his commune only when she knew that he had impregnated her.

Frank Laughlin, then attending art school in Boston, was her lover. She returned and told him that she had forgotten to take her pill on the passionate eve of her departure for California. Delighted, Frank repeated his proposal of marriage. She pretended to relent by slow degrees, and they were married within a week. Patrick, named for Frank's grandfather, was born eight months later.

When her secret nightmare proved groundless, and Patrick was not born as a retarded albino with twelve toes, she realized that she was happy, outrageously so. She had exorcised her childhood demons, she had spat in the face of taboo and repression, and she had produced a son by the man she loved most on earth. She loved her husband, too, in a quieter and more comfortable way. Frank had a promising career, he could be terribly witty, they shared many interests.

But things went wrong somewhere. She had plenty of opportunity over the years to see that Frank's nasty, small-minded intervention in her program for Patrick's upbringing had been no momentary aberration. His behavior tonight had illustrated his neurotic confusion about sex. He was probably terrified by his fascination with Alfred Roberts, and so he raged and blustered about his costume. It was just one more twist in a fantastically intricate escape-route from the fact of his natural, physical self. Frank had no idea at all why he acted the way he did, why he said the things he said.

When the music from the Hall stopped for a moment, she heard a noise at the door behind her. At first she thought it was the blowing rain, but the noise was too regular and persistent. The music started again, drowning the feeble sound. She got up and bent her head close to the door. Something was scratching against the outside.

She felt a sudden and unreasonable fear. She turned to reassure herself that the room was full of people, that the fire burned brightly on the hearth, before she could bring herself to open the door a crack. A girl in white stood in the gloom.

"Good heavens, why didn't you ring the bell? Come inside."

"I didn't want to disturb anyone else."

Rose observed that her feet and legs were bare, despite the cold. They were bruised and scratched and muddy. Her hair might have been blond, but it was darkened and plastered tightly to her skull by the rain. Her determined self-neglect and the vacant innocence of her stare suggested some of the strays she had met at her father's commune. But all of them would be much older now.

Rose gestured impatiently. "Come in."

"No. Can you come out for a minute?"

"Me?" She let one absurd question hang in the air for a minute before asking another: "Are you one of Patrick's friends?"

"I want to see Rose Laughlin. That's you, isn't it?"

The girl's manner was distant, detached. She seemed as unmindful of the cold and the wet as she was of the strangeness of her errand. She didn't look drugged, but Rose assumed that she must be; unless she had just strolled over from the nearby cemetery.

"Yes. Please come in. There's a fire just inside. We're having a party. . . ."

Unspeaking, the girl drifted back out of the light. Rose felt compelled to follow her and coax her inside, although she had deep misgivings. Her flippant thought about the cemetery now seemed less funny. Soon the rain was beating down on her own head and the girl was just a blur in the darkness.

"Please —"

"I have a message from your father."

"What? Is this a joke, like those costumes? Are you another one of Howie's — one of Dr. Ashcroft's friends? I'm really in no mood for this nonsense."

"He begs you to claim your inheritance before it's too late. You are being betrayed in your own home. There is no one you can trust, no one can depend upon. You must take the power. You must use it."

Her voice faded as the speech progressed. Her form receded. Rose lunged forward, but she could now see nothing of the girl.

"Rose? Mrs. Laughlin, is that you out here?"

She whirled to find the Scarecrow silhouetted in the door. The coincidence seemed too great. She stalked forward, planning to shake a confession out of him if she had to.

"Clearing your head? I could use some air myself. Shall I get your coat —"

"Who the hell was *that?*"

He shook his head and looked genuinely bewildered. She lost some of her confidence. "That girl who just came to the door, the scrawny blond?"

"I didn't see anyone. I just this minute got here. Is there any reason why I should know her? Did she ask for me?"

"No, I'm sorry, it was . . . I guess it was meant to be a kind of joke."

She realized that Ashcroft couldn't have been responsible for the bizarre visitation. She had told no one but Patrick of her dreams about the cellar, and she hadn't even told him that her father played a part in them. She was reluctant to accept the notion that the girl was a daughter of one of her father's former disciples — perhaps even her own half-sister. Did those people still linger on the mountaintop, revering his memory? She didn't want to know. If that was where she came from, it would mean accepting that the dreams were real messages from her dead father. But the only alternative — that she had been hallucinating — was even less acceptable.

"Please, come in and let me close the door. You don't look well. I don't know why you and your husband have come to the conclusion that I'm the neighborhood prankster — although, now that I think of it, it shows a rather sophisticated understanding of my faith. The Devil is supposed to be the Father of Lies, and all jokes are lies of a sort. Perhaps that's why our adversaries are so humorless, and why our First Parents seem like such a dreary couple. Can you imagine Adam giving Eve a dribble-glass, or her rigging his chair with a whoopee-cushion?"

Rose was amazed to find herself capable of laughter, the kind that forced her to hang onto his arm to keep from doubling over: probably a nervous reaction to her shock, but it felt good. With his style, his timing, his delivery, Ashcroft was an amusing man. Unless she had been misreading his ironic tone from the first, she suspected that he saw his religion merely as a way of making money, attracting attention, and shocking the sort of people who read grocery-store tabloids. She was intensely grateful that he was the first person to speak to her after her interview with the weird girl. If she had met Jane Miniter, for instance, and become enmeshed in one of her conversations, she would be in a straitjacket by now.

"Odd things happen here, don't they?" Seeing that she wasn't about to answer, he went on: "Your son has been telling me a curious story."

"Oh?" She hoped that Patrick hadn't been telling him about her obsession with the cellar, but she could think of no other "curious" story he might have told. The girl had warned her that she was being betrayed — but she cut off that line of speculation.

"Yes, it seems he had a dream about a woman, an especially forceful woman, someone he thinks may have been associated with this place in the past."

"You mean, a ghost? He didn't tell me anything about it."

"Well, I hope I'm not — no, he didn't swear me to secrecy. And the word 'ghost' wasn't mentioned, but I suppose it was implied."

"What was so curious about the dream?"

"Nothing." He was obviously pleased to keep her in suspense for a moment before adding: "The curiosity was a sequel to the dream. He later saw a sketch of the same woman in his father's studio. When Patrick asked who the model had been, Frank said he didn't know, that her features had come to him in a flash of inspiration."

"That *is* odd, isn't it! And I can't think why he didn't tell me about it, we've always been very close. I wonder — people who meet you, some of them, often tell you about their experiences with demonic possession, or precognition, or how their Aunt Fannie was a reincarnation of Cleopatra, don't they?"

"That, alas, is all too true. But I don't think your son was just trying to make interesting conversation. Nor do I think he was trying to put me on. He was obviously shaken by the coincidence. And there was one detail — it's hardly conclusive of anything, but he was quite impressed by his dream-girl's red hair. Your ancestor had a partner in his deviltry, his daughter, a woman named Mirdath, whose red hair was widely . . . well, not admired, since everyone hated her guts, but it certainly drew attention. By all accounts, she was the brains of the outfit." His tone had regained its irony, and he added as if it were high praise indeed: "She was a thoroughly reprehensible character."

"Well, what do you think of it?" she asked when he gave no sign of continuing. "Is she haunting our house?"

He shrugged. "I have no idea. For all I know, she's not even dead. There was some confusion about her eventual fate."

"Oh, come *on!*"

"Mordred was supposed to be at least three hundred years old when he died, hadn't you heard that? A man named Mordred Glendower was secretary to Dr. John Dee in the reign of Elizabeth I, and he earned a rather evil reputation. His notoriety in London was such that Shakespeare was no doubt making a topical joke when he referred to 'the great magician, damned Glendower.'"

"You can't believe that he was the same man who built this mill."

"No, I suppose not. But you aren't going to get me to admit that it's impossible. That would take all the fun out of my religion."

"And you also think it's possible that Mirdath is still hiding in the cellar?" She hadn't considered those words, and she felt a shiver as she spoke them. She tried to drown out their aftertaste by continuing hastily, "How could I find out more about — about those people?"

"I could tell you what little I know and lend you some books. Perhaps a look at your husband's sketch would be revealing. I don't know what it could tell us, but I'd like to see it."

"So would I. Where's Frank? Have you seen him lately?"

"I've been looking for him for an hour without any success. Perhaps he got bored with the party and went to work in his studio. I've known artists —"

"He's probably just passed out somewhere," she said shortly. "We don't need his permission to look, though. He's not at all secretive about his work."

Leading the way, she wondered if that were entirely true. She had to admit she wouldn't usually have invited a stranger to look at Frank's work. Perhaps her motive was pure spite. She hesitated at the foot of the stairs as she tried to spot Frank in the crowd. She couldn't. She saw Patrick on the far side of the room, closely followed by someone as tall and thin as he was, made up quite imaginatively as a desiccated corpse. Oddly, they were both limping.

She turned to climb the stairs, unable to contain her curiosity. Some of her annoyance with Frank overflowed toward Patrick. She couldn't understand why he had kept the odd occurrence secret from her — worse, why he had excluded her from a secret he apparently shared with Frank. His failure to confide in her may have been what her visitor meant by a betrayal.

The noise of the party followed them, seeming even louder at the top of the stairs: Iggy Pop, now, and *Lust for Life*. "Mirdath's theme-song," Ashcroft murmured.

She tugged at his sleeve sharply, as much to register her displeasure as to direct him toward the door of the studio. The dim glow from Frank's skylight showed that the door stood ajar.

She walked in and snapped on the light. Two bare bodies, writhing on the couch, froze at the same instant she did. She had taken a step back, mumbling apologetically, before she saw that the one on top was Frank. His pale bulk largely concealed the woman he was taking from the rear. He stared dumbly for a moment, and then terror flickered across his beefy face.

Rose saw that she had made a mistake. She hadn't surprised her husband with another woman. He had been buggering Alfred Roberts.

Chapter Seven

"Sounds like a heavy trip," said Bill Kraft, who salted his speech with archaic slang when he spoke to young persons.

Patrick sat with him and Amy at the kitchen table. He would have preferred to exclude Amy, but she was now as much a fixture of the place as the sink or the refrigerator, and he wanted to talk to Bill away from the distractions of the party.

The psychologist gnawed his lower lip with his wax fangs for a moment and then sipped his drink before he said: "But the explanation could be very simple."

"I'd like to hear it."

"Well —" Bill laughed — "I'm still thinking it up. All right, try this: the creative process and the dream process are similar. Nobody ever really creates anything. They pick and choose from their experiences and reassemble the pieces in new ways. And by experiences, I mean not only what they've done, but everything they've seen or read or heard about, every movie or book or television program that's come their way. Can you dig it?"

"I follow you," Patrick said.

"What a lousy way to look at Van Gogh!" Amy said.

"No, it isn't. I'm not saying there's no such thing as genius. If there wasn't, everybody would paint like Van Gogh, or nobody would. All I'm saying is, he had to work with the totality of his experience, and nothing more. He wasn't taking dictation from some outside source.

"Now, to get back to your case," he said to Patrick. "You and your father have shared many experiences. You've gone to many of the same movies, looked at the same pictures, met the same people. More to the point, you've been looking at your father's pictures all your life. You know his style, you know the type of woman he likes to paint, the lighting he prefers, the features that he tends to play down or accentuate. It's no big deal that your dream and his creation should share a family resemblance."

"But Patrick said it was more than a resemblance," Amy said. "He said it was the same woman."

"Okay, but memory is tricky. Images in dreams are imprecise. And here we're talking about Patrick's memory of an image in a dream. How vague can you get? So, recognizing a couple of understandable points of similarity, you say, 'Aha! It's her!'"

"But my image of her was clearer than that, as clear —"

"Yeah, it seems that way now, but maybe that's a judgment after the fact. Your image could have been fuzzy until the moment you saw the picture. Seeing it crystallized the image in your mind. Haven't you ever experienced déjà-vu?"

"Sure."

"My mother had an aunt who —" Amy began.

Bill overrode her: "There are several theories of what causes it. The most plausible — to me, anyway — is that your senses are momentarily out of synch with your brain. You see or hear or taste something a split second before your conscious mind is aware of the stimulus. So that you just *know* that you've been there before — and you have been, except that you weren't there in some previous life, you were there a split second ago without being aware of it. That may have happened to you. In the brief fraction of time when your conscious mind was out to lunch, your subconscious was taking in the picture and shuffling your dream-memories to match it. Then your conscious mind got back in step and you were hit by the shock of recognition, by an extreme case of déjà-vu."

"Is that really possible?" Patrick asked slowly.

"The human mind is infinitely complex, and it spends a lot of its free time playing tricks on itself," Bill said, with the air of someone quoting himself. "*Anything* is possible — except, if you'll forgive me, some of the explanations you suggested. The theory that somebody gave both you and your father a post-hypnotic suggestion — that's possible, but the only person who'd take it seriously is somebody who thinks that the FBI is controlling his thoughts by shooting laser beams through his television set. As for telepathy, or ghosts, forget about it, there ain't no such animals."

"You can't just sit there and say that without proof!" Amy cried.

"Aristotle himself couldn't sit here and prove a negative proposition." Bill proceeded to give her a short course in logic, which Amy rejected volubly.

Patrick ignored their argument as he considered whether or not to tell Bill about the baby. He never read the local paper; their only television set was the one in Frank's studio; he had no friends who chatted with him about local sensations: so that tonight was the first he had heard about the discovery of a dead infant near the Miniter house. Bill had come within an inch of convincing him on the other question, and he would have liked to hear him try to explain away the cannibal feast, but he didn't dare. He believed that Bill would have no choice but to conclude that he was a lunatic and a murderer.

He hadn't mentioned it to Howard Ashcroft, either. He knew that Amy's mother had directed the police to his house after her discovery, and Patrick didn't want to appear to be fishing for idle gossip. But Ashcroft, if he got to know him better, might be a good choice as a confidant. Unlike Bill, he had accepted the story of the dream-picture at face value and had offered no glib explanation. In fact he had offered no explanation at all. Disconcertingly, he had seized Patrick's shoulder and gravely advised him to get himself and his parents away from the mill as soon as possible. He would say no more, except to press upon Patrick an invitation to come to his Sabbat on Tuesday night. Patrick had resolved to go, if only to further his acquaintance with Justine d'Estranges.

". . . so to get back to your problem," Bill was saying as he rose from the table and patted his fright-wig into place, "if you want my advice, you'll accept what happened as a queer trick that a healthy mind played on itself, and stop brooding about it. If you want to discuss it some more, why don't you drop by my office some day after school? It'll be on the house. Look, I better get back to the old lady. It was fun rapping with you guys."

"It was groovy," Amy said with a perfectly straight face. When he had left, she breathed to Patrick, "What an asshole!"

He shared her laughter as their eyes met for a moment. He felt completely at ease with her, and he'd never felt that way before with a girl his own age. The realization made him self-conscious, and he averted his eyes at the same instant she did, as if they had both responded to a prearranged signal.

The silence became oppressive, and he was glad when she broke it. "You should talk to Dr. Ashcroft. I bet he wouldn't try to explain everything away with a lot of doubletalk."

"I did ask him, and he wasn't much help. All he did was invite me to his Sabbat on Tuesday night."

"His what?"

"A Sabbat. A get-together for witches, a Black Mass."

Amy laughed. "He invited me, too, only he just called it a Hallowe'en party. He was very nice. He was the first older person who didn't try to drag me out into that snake pit to *have fun,* yuck! He just talked for a while and then asked me to his party. I never even met him before."

"You suppose you'll go?"

"I want to. It's the first time anybody besides a relative ever asked me anywhere by myself." She paused for a moment, frowning. "But it's a school night. And my mother thinks he's weird."

Patrick stared at her for a moment, then blurted: "Are you a virgin?"

"Huh? I *beg* your pardon!" Her voice rose to a squeak as her face reddened. "If you must know, yes, not that it's any of your business. What kind of a question is that?"

"Please don't get upset. It's just that a funny thought occurred to me."

She watched him sidelong as she fought a smile. "What kind of a funny thought?"

"I don't know how serious Dr. Ashcroft is about this Satanism-business, or how closely he sticks to the traditional script, but according to what I've read, the Satanists need a virgin for their ceremony. They use her body for an altar."

"You mean, like her *naked* body?" She giggled. "So?"

"What happens is, according to the books, they involve her in an orgy and use her every whichway."

When he got up the nerve to look at her again, she seemed surprisingly unperturbed. He added, "Whether she wants to or not." That also failed to alarm her.

"Are you going?"

"I think so."

"Well, aren't you a virgin, too?"

He waved a dismissive hand. "Boys don't count. It's the symbolic significance, you know, of breaking into something for the first time."

She began to giggle. She whispered, almost inaudibly: "Do you want to save me from a fate worse than death?"

"I don't understand."

"Well, if I'm not still a virgin anymore when I go there. . . ." Her voice trailed off as she studied him with terrifying earnestness.

He was appalled. His desire for a woman was always with him nowadays, like a wasting disease. The surest cure would have been the redhaired woman; but since she didn't exist outside of dreams and pictures, he would have settled for a reasonable substitute, like Shana Jennings or Justine. The thought of making love to Amy Miniter had never entered his head. His soul cringed with embarrassment as he saw there was no kind way he could refuse her. Compounding his confusion, the naked directness of her offer had provoked a stir of response. He noticed for the first time, too, that she wasn't all that bad.

She studied the aimless movement of her own fingers on the table as she said, "Don't look so scared. I was only trying to make a joke." To prove this, she forced out a ghastly little laugh. "I guess it wasn't very funny. Anyway, I know you've got a thing for that skinny girl."

"I . . . what?"

"I saw you dancing with her two or three times. You were looking at her the way Lance looks at me whenever I open the fridge."

"Lance?"

"One of our dogs. How could you go for somebody like that?"

He stared at her, totally baffled. He had indeed taken a stab at dancing two or three times, but only with Justine. Amy, despite her professed disdain for the snake pit, must have been peeking at him from the kitchen door.

"What do you mean, how could I go for her? She looks. . . ."

He could find no words, but she supplied some: "Like she needs a *bath*, for heaven's sake! Her hair's all stringy and tangled, she's even thinner than you are, she looks like she never heard of a comb or a toothbrush. I bet she smells bad. I know I'm not the best-looking girl in the world, but at least I'm *developed.*" She gestured impulsively toward her breasts, then blushed and looked away.

"Amy — you're not talking about the blond in the backless white thing —"

"Yes! The one with all the scratches and hickeys on her legs!" she cried vehemently. "There are two of them with the same kind of outfit, your father's friend from New York, who's very pretty, in the black outfit, and that beanpole with the green teeth in the white one. Honestly, Patrick, I know I'm kind of plain, but I'm not stupid or blind, and I *know* I'm better looking than she is. Just because she's hardly got any clothes on —"

He could stand no more of this venomous tirade. He had come to like Amy. Underneath her mousy exterior she had seemed to be humorous and sensitive and intelligent. But once he had rejected her offer, she revealed a streak of viciousness that bordered on insanity. She actually seemed to believe her own transparent slanders.

"I ought to get back," he said, getting up and backing toward the door.

"I'm looking forward to Dr. Ashcroft's party. Maybe I'll see you there."

He slipped out. The more he thought about it, the funnier it seemed: Amy Miniter as the virginal centerpiece of a Black Mass. Virgins must be scarce nowadays, and the handful of misfits and outcasts who deluded themselves into practicing demonolatry had to make do with what they could find. He began to laugh, but then he was assaulted by a vivid image of Amy, nude and supine. Her pale skin was smooth and tight-textured. Her breasts were large. If he hadn't been so damned picky — but perhaps the word was cowardly — he could even now have been caressing her breasts and feeling her slim legs as they pressed his ribs, while he —

In his confusion he blundered into the Ashcroft bat. The bat, a portly man in a black, big-eared hood that covered the upper half of his face, grinned as if expecting recognition.

"Excuse me," Patrick said.

"You don't know me, do you, Patrick? I've been looking for you to say hello, but you're never around. I met your father earlier, but now he's disappeared. So has your mother. I got to admit it's a novel idea for a party: invite a lot of people you don't know, then run and hide."

The whining, nasal voice was unmistakable, but Patrick found it hard to credit the identification. It was Mr. Bamberger, his English teacher, whom he detested. The feeling was reciprocated, but only impersonally. Bamberger disliked all his students as an extension of the dislike he felt for his job.

"How are you, Mr. Bamberger?"

"Listen, Patrick, anytime you see me dressed as a bat with a glass of scotch in my hand, you can call me Bob, is that a deal?"

"I didn't know you were a friend of Dr. Ashcroft's, Bob."

"Friend? I'm a student, a follower. I think his theories are fascinating. More importantly, they work."

"Aye, but his work is to change smocksniffs into sodomites and cast glamours on serving-wenches," Patrick laughed. "To call upon the Great Old Ones is no pastime for mountebanks."

"Huh? Is that some literary allusion I ought to know?"

"Why . . . no, I was just kidding around, talking off the top of my head." Patrick tried to conceal his embarrassment. He hadn't meant to say anything like that, whatever it meant. Odd words and strange accents had come from his mouth without premeditation more than once tonight. He hastened to continue: "Do you attend his Sabbats, and so forth?"

"Oh, sure, yeah, that's the best part. I never realized what parameters I'd imposed upon my lifestyle until —"

"Where's the fucking ice? You got any ice, kid?"

The urgency, the desperation of the voice didn't fit the question, and Patrick gave the speaker his immediate attention. It was a man costumed as a hood from the fifties, in black leather jacket and mirror sunglasses. Patrick had seen him with the woman who had duplicated Justine's costume in black.

"Yes, on the bar —"

"You got fucking *nothing* over there. Come on, man, this is an emergency!"

"Come with me." Patrick led the way to the kitchen. "What's the matter?"

"Alfred got her face bashed in, that's the matter. I told her she was crazy, going in drag to some square party out in the sticks, but when did she ever listen to me? Now she wants to call the cops, the dumb cunt, but I think I talked her out of it. Come on, ice, ice, *ice!*"

This explanation only served to arouse Patrick's curiosity, but since the man was now literally dancing with impatience, he suppressed it and hurried to pull two plastic bags of icecubes from the freezer. The man seized one and fled. Patrick decided to take the other to the bar, since no one else seemed to be playing host.

"What happened?" Amy asked.

"Damned if I know. Did you notice anybody in drag tonight?"

"Maybe it was that girl you were dancing with."

Patrick ignored that and left as quickly as his limp would allow.

He couldn't explain the limp. The impulse — no, it wasn't just an impulse, it was a necessity, his leg actually pained him from time to time — whatever it was, it had come upon him when he donned the costume. Maybe he had traded good vision for a bad leg. It was hard to believe that he wasn't wearing his glasses and that one eye was covered by a patch. He could make out the features of every person in the vast, dim room — including those of Shana Jennings.

He dropped the bag of ice on the bar and hurried toward her. She stood at the entrance to the room, surveying the crowd and laughing. He saw now that she was laughing with her boyfriend, Bruce Curtis, and another youth. Patrick slowed his pace, but he didn't stop.

"Hello, Shana. I'm glad you could come after all."

"Patrick, this is really, really weird. I didn't think that even you could come up with something so weird. Look at all those crazies! Wow!"

"Why didn't you wear a costume?"

"What do you think we are, a bunch of assholes?" Bruce said, and the others laughed.

"I hope you don't mind that I brought a couple of friends, Patrick. You told me I could bring some, right?" Her smile was unusually vacant.

"Sure, that's fine. Make yourselves at home."

"Here? Jesus Christ!" Bruce said, touching off more laughter. "Where's the booze?"

"We haven't met," Patrick said, extending his hand. "My name's Patrick Laughlin."

Bruce ignored him. Having spotted the bar, he brushed past Patrick's outstretched hand and swaggered toward it with his hulking friend.

"Don't mind him, Patrick," Shana said. "He's drunk. I'm stoned. What're you?"

If I took this fuddled baggage to the cellar and swyved her, Patrick thought, none would be the wiser, neither her sodden swain nor any of these rabble. He took her arm, intending to do just that, when he came to his senses. He wondered how he knew that "swyve" meant "fuck." He couldn't recall encountering that word before.

"You better not grab me like that when Bruce is around. Of course, when he's not around. . . ."

Patrick smiled, pleased with himself for not rising to that bait. He could see that she was merely amusing herself, and he wondered why he had been so blind in the past. He let go of her arm as he noticed a commotion in the crowd. A group led by the man in the leather jacket and the blond in the black body-stocking was pushing its way forward from the stairs.

"Excuse me." He moved away from Shana.

"Where's Amy? That's what we came to see."

He tried to ignore the question, but he found that he couldn't. He turned and said, "I don't know, I think she went home."

"Oh, shit."

The girl dressed as Hecate held a towel filled with icecubes to her mouth. Her nose was swollen, her eyes were purplish slits. The hoodlum comforted her. Their feathered and sequined cohorts fluttered and exclaimed around them.

"Can I help?" Patrick asked. "Can I do anything for you?"

Hecate stopped the parade short. She lowered the towel and glared at him. Her lips were split and swollen. "Yes, dear, you can," she snarled. "You can tell your rotten pig of a father that he's washed up in New York if I have anything to say about it, and by God, I do! Tell him he'd better look for a job plastering billboards in Duluth."

She wanted to sweep on by, but he blocked her. Or was this a man? That seemed incredible, even though the voice was deep and he had been told the victim was in drag.

"Frank didn't hit you, did he?"

"He hit *on* me, darling, and then he put on a show of outrage for the little woman. Or maybe that part had been programmed, and they were both getting their rocks off on some freaky S-M trip. I don't know. I don't want to know. Get out of my way!"

Patrick stepped aside to let them make their exit. Other guests immediately surrounded him with questions. "She slipped and fell in the bathroom," he kept repeating as he tried to work his way toward the stairs.

"Patrick, we must be off," George Spencer said. "Where are your parents?"

"There was some kind of accident upstairs, and I suppose they're cleaning up. A woman fell and hurt herself in the bathroom, nothing serious. I'm sure they'll understand if you leave without saying goodnight."

"Someone ought to," George said. "Rupert ran off without a word."

"But it was a marvelous party," Madge said. "Give them my love, Patrick."

Others followed the Spencers' lead. Patrick felt bound to stand in for his parents in accepting the farewells and compliments and helping to find coats and purses. even though he wished passionately that they would all just leave and let him find out what had happened upstairs. He knew that his father despised homosexuals, and he couldn't imagine him *hitting on* one. Or hitting one, either. Frank might be a bigot, but his bigotry went not much further than grumbling at his television set.

He tried to recall the strange words he had been compelled to speak to Mr. Bamberger. He had said that Ashcroft's powers only worked for changing smocksniffs into sodomites. In Elizabethan slang, a smocksniff was a womanizer, and Frank was surely that. He had said something, too, about casting glamors on serving-wenches. A glamor was a magical spell that could delude you about someone's appearance. Merlin had pulled that trick in the Arthurian legends. Was the magnificent Justine d'Estranges really a beanpole with green teeth and hickeys on her legs?

Of course not. He had probably spoken those strange words because someone had slipped something into the punch. Amy's assessment of Justine was malicious nonsense. Hell hath no fury, etc.

At last the first wave of departures seemed to have spent itself, leaving the Hall still crowded. He began to thread his way again toward the stairs when he saw another developing crisis: Shana and Bruce and their large, shaggy friend were just entering the kitchen. He supposed he couldn't stop them from tormenting Amy, but he might be able to draw away some of their fire. He felt responsible for her.

Entering the kitchen, he was relieved to find Mr. Bamberger there. As an adult and a teacher, he might exert a stabilizing influence. Then he observed Mr. Bamberger's clenched jaw, clenched fists, and white face. The man was terrified.

"Hey, here's the top honcho himself!" Bruce cried, slinging a heavy arm around Patrick's narrow shoulders and dragging him further into the room. "I hate to break the news to you, dude, but we came in here and found Hamburger making out with your chick."

"It's not true, Patrick!" Amy cried. "We were sitting here and talking, that was all."

Thanks a lot, Amy! For all he cared, Bamberger could have been screwing her on the kitchen table, but her spontaneous outburst made it seem as if he did care.

"Why do you call him Hamburger? He looks more like a Batburger," suggested Bruce's friend. He wore a greasy down vest that bared arms as thick as most men's thighs. He held a quart of vodka in one hand and a joint in the other. "Do you suppose, if we threw him out the window, he would fly?"

"Now wait a minute," Bamberger began, half-rising, but Shana swayed against him and weighed him down into his chair. Terrified though he might be, he seemed to like this.

"Don't you be scared, Bobby," she crooned, stroking his cheek. "I won't let them throw you out the window, you're too cute."

"We're on the ground floor, Bob," Patrick said.

"Hey! We can always drag the silly cocksucker upstairs," Bruce said, still holding Patrick and apparently needing the support. "I got to hand it to you, dude, I never seen such a bunch of wimps and pussies and pigs at one party in my entire life. And right here, in this fucking kitchen, we got three people who . . . what's the word, Patrick, when you got a small piece of something that stands for the whole fucking mess?"

"A microcosm."

"Jesus Christ, listen to that!" Bruce crowed. "Did you hear that, Duke? Didn't I tell you that this was one brainy motherfucker? Say that word again for Duke, Patrick, he's kind of slow."

"Microcosm."

"Shit," said Duke, shaking his shaggy head slowly and then taking a long pull from his bottle.

"So, what am I saying? Yeah, here we got a microcosm — a wimp, a pussy, and a pig."

"Which is which?" Shana asked, still snuggling against Bamberger and now beginning to rotate her hips slowly in his lap.

"Hamburger, it's your turn," Bruce said, stumbling as he dragged Patrick with him toward the teacher. "Tell me the word for what she's being."

"I — I don't understand."

"Fucking-A you don't, you're just a fucking Hamburger. Now listen to me, and stamp your foot twice if you understand. Stop playing with his dick, Shana, you filthy cunt, he got to concentrate. When somebody knows the answer to something, like you do to my question, only they act like a wise-ass and pretend they don't know, what do you call it when they do that?"

"I don't know," Bamberger muttered. "I don't know what you mean."

"Listen to that, a fucking English teacher. Patrick knows. Tell us, Patrick."

"Disingenuous."

Bruce let go of him at last so he could lurch to the table and brace himself there, shaking his head slowly, miming a man trying to recover his wits after a staggering blow.

"My God. Did you hear that one? Did you hear that, Duke?"

Duke belched at great length.

"You took the words out of my mouth, Duke. *Dis-in-gen-u-ous*. Now don't be disingenuous with us, Hamburger. Which is which?"

"What?" Bamberger said.

Now that he was free, Patrick walked to the table and sat on it near Amy's chair. He winked at her, then wondered if the signal could be interpreted when he was wearing an eyepatch. She appeared to understand. She smiled shyly.

His own detachment surprised him. He was mildly amused by Bruce's insults, nothing more. He knew that the two drunken goons might prove dangerous, but he didn't share in Bamberger's terror. He had been through worse experiences lately. His descent into the cellar the other day had scared him more than these two ever could.

"I'm losing my patience with you," Bruce said to Bamberger. "I'll tell Shana to stop giving you a dry fuck if you don't shape up. I'll let Duke give you a flying lesson, how would you like that? Okay, now. I said that here we got a microcosm of the party, on account of we got a wimp, a pussy, and a pig. Now, which is which? And if you say, 'I don't know,' I'm gonna bash you."

Bamberger's mouth worked silently. Sweat trickled down his jowls. Writhing in his lap, Shana continued to stroke his chest and his bat-eared head in an obscene parody of affection.

"We'll narrow it down." Bruce leaned forward from the waist until his eyes were inches from the teacher's mask. "Which one are you?"

"Bruce," Patrick said, "why don't you all go out and have another drink? You —"

"Shut up!" Bruce barked without turning. Bamberger was so jolted that his chair rattled beneath him. "I'm waiting, Hamburger."

"I — the wimp?"

"Wrong!" Bruce screamed in his face. "Wrong! You get one more chance. And this time, Mr. English Teacher, you will answer in a complete sentence. 'I am a. . . .'"

Patrick was annoyed with Amy for reaching out and gripping his hand. It would only give the bullies something more to mock. But he didn't withdraw his hand. Hers was dry and cool.

"I am a . . . pussy," Bamberger choked.

"Get him to sign it, and I'll pin it up in the girls' lavatory," Shana said.

"That's a good idea, Shana. Whoever said you were an empty-headed slut?"

"You did."

"Well, I take it back. You're almost as smart as Pat-prick. Hey, I hear you make poor Shana pat your prick in study hall so she can copy your homework. That sounds like a clear case of sexual harassment to me. Isn't that right, Pat-prick?"

Patrick was annoyed to feel his face burn. He hadn't wanted Amy to hear that, and he looked away from her. But she surprised him by squeezing his hand in sympathy for his embarrassment. He mumbled, "If you say so."

"'If you say so,'" Bruce simpered. Everything that he did convulsed his friends with laughter. Shana laughed the loudest.

Bruce turned to Amy, leaning toward her over the table. "Now, we all know which one you are, but we want to hear it straight from the pig's mouth. What are you?"

She took her hand from Patrick's and shrank back in her chair. Bruce leaned closer. Her large eyes grew even larger, until her pale face seemed to fade around them.

"Say it, Amy." Bruce's tone was mockingly soothing.

Patrick felt helpless, like one watching a cliff begin to crumble above him. He knew that it would be disastrous to lose his temper, but he was losing it more completely than he'd ever done before. He felt an unfamiliar, cold tingle in his extremities. He began to rock from side to side as he fought to control himself.

"Say it, Amy."

Not at all as Bamberger had mumbled, Amy cried loudly and clearly: "Bruce Curtis, you are a pig!"

Shana shrieked with laughter. Bruce drew back his hand and slapped Amy across the face. The report was still ringing in the room when Patrick sprang. He drove his fist into Bruce's ear with all his force. Bruce staggered back, clutching the side of his head. He tripped and sprawled on his back. Patrick heard Duke and Shana laughing as he flung himself on Bruce and seized his throat.

Patrick's advantage was brief. Bruce pulled his hands away from his throat easily. Despite Patrick's desperate efforts to hold him down, he sat up, then stood up. He shoved Patrick back against the table. A sudden numbness in his back gave way to the worst pain he had ever felt. The pain didn't keep that distinction for long. It surrendered its place when Bruce hit him in the stomach. He tried to breathe, but his lungs were paralyzed. He heard Amy screaming as the stone floor rushed up at his face.

Patrick rolled over on his back. He tasted blood. Compared with the emotion that now filled him, his previous anger seemed only a fit of pique. The swinish clotpoll that now stood astride him had dared to lay his hands upon a Master of the Runes! He stretched forth a trembling hand and gasped the First of the Ten Words that are the Litany of Hastur.

Bruce's lips stretched back from his teeth in a horrifying rictus. He uttered a piercing scream. His eyes rolled back in their sockets until only the whites showed. Bright red drops burst from his nose and ears before he fell, and then his heels and his skull beat a clattering tattoo on the floor as his body quivered in an arch that seemed to defy the laws of human physiology.

"Holy fuck, he's throwing a fit! Don't let him swallow his tongue," Duke said, but not even he moved to implement the suggestion.

By the time Patrick had pulled himself to his feet, gripping the table for support, Bruce lay still. Except for the trickles of blood, he was the color of wax. The red bubbles forming occasionally at his mouth were the only sign that he was breathing.

Patrick cleared his throat and said, "You'd better get him to a doctor."

"That one punch got him just right," Duke said admiringly. "You damn near killed the poor bastard." He screwed up his face, waved a big hand in front of it. "He even shit himself."

Shana had dismounted from Mr. Bamberger's lap. Sucking one of her knuckles, she stared at Patrick. She seemed unable to stop giggling.

"Okay, Shana, 'I am a wimp.' Now are you happy? Get the hell out of here!"

"Should I pick him up?" Duke asked Mr. Bamberger. "Do you think I should move him?"

"I don't know. I think I should call the police. I think I should call the police and have you hoodlums prosecuted to the fullest extent of the law. Trespassing — threatening — assault — calling me dirty names —"

"I didn't do nothing!" Duke protested.

"Forget it, Bob," Patrick said, "please. It was my fault. I invited them. I'm sorry."

"Little bastards," Bamberger growled, trudging from the room. He threw over his shoulder: "And how dare you call me 'Bob'?"

With obvious disgust at the smell, Duke picked up Bruce and slung him over his shoulder. Shana followed him out the door, backing out, still gnawing her knuckle as she stared at Patrick. At the last moment she spun and ran through the door.

Patrick turned to Amy and was surprised to see her staring at him much as Shana had. He said, "Are you all right?"

"What did you say?" she whispered.

"I said, are you —"

"No — before — it was like a hand grabbed him and squeezed him and flung him down on the floor. It wasn't like he just fell down in a fit, it was like . . . something . . . *seized* him."

"Well, that must be why they've always called it a *seizure.*"

He suspected the explanation was lame, but she gave it some thought. Then she said: "Just before it happened, you said something."

"I didn't say anything. I couldn't say anything. *Gaaack*, maybe, that's about all I could have managed. I was just trying to breathe. He had an epileptic seizure, that's all."

She shocked him by springing to her feet and hurling herself upon him. Standing on tiptoe, she grabbed his neck with both hands and pulled his head down. She kissed him as if she were trying to eat his teeth. Just when he realized that he was kissing a real girl for the first time, just as he became aware of the pressure of her breasts and the taut resiliency of her thighs, she pulled away.

"I'm sorry," she said.

He had no idea what to say. He couldn't wipe off what felt like an incredibly foolish grin.

"That was the bravest thing I ever saw, hitting a huge thug like that. That was wonderful."

"Telling him he was a pig was even braver."

"No, it wasn't. I just lost my temper."

"So did I." They both laughed. Then they stopped laughing and stared at each other in wild speculation.

Patrick hurried to break the silence. "My father — something happened upstairs. I was on my way to check —" he moved back toward the door —

"when I got sidetracked. I want to —"

Jane Miniter burst through the door, blocking his exit.

"What's going on in here? This party is starting to look like the last act of *Hamlet*. Every time I turn around, a body smeared with gore is being hauled out. What happened? Bob Bamberger said you were all held captive and terrorized by a dozen hooligans with brass knuckles and motorcycle chains, but I don't believe a word that man says. Did you know that he has the nerve to call himself a *witch* while he worships Satan? The so-called witches were followers of the Old Religion, women who worshipped the all-giving Earth Mother. They were of course persecuted by narrow-minded men who envied their sisterhood and tried to pin all that Devil-worship and naked orgy nonsense on them. For a man to call himself a witch is as ridiculous as . . . as ridiculous as Bob Bamberger calling himself a teacher. But he won't be one for long, not after the Board of Education hears what I heard tonight. Well, why won't you speak up? Why doesn't someone say something?"

Both Miniters stared at him. He couldn't detect a hint of Amy's future appearance in her bull-headed, bulgy-eyed mother, but maybe he was deluding himself. He said, "I got into a stupid fight, that's all, with someone from school. He had too much to drink. He was insulting Bob and Amy and me, and one thing led to another. I was losing the fight pretty badly when he threw some kind of fit."

"It wasn't like that at all, Mama! Bruce had us all scared silly, all except Patrick. And Bruce had a friend who was twice as big as he was, who drank gin straight out of a bottle and wanted to throw Mr. Bamberger through a window. Mr. Bamberger almost shit a brick, so he did everything they told him to. So then Bruce, he was the worst one, except for the horrible, slutty girl who egged them on, Bruce slapped me, and Patrick knocked him down with one punch. It was wonderful! Then when they were fighting, he started to foam at the mouth and bleed out of his ears and everything, because Patrick had hit him so hard."

"Good heavens, Patrick, I must admit I never dreamed you had it in you." Before he could acknowledge that questionable compliment, she rounded on her daughter: "Nor you, either, young lady. Since when did you start using that kind of language? I was foolish in believing that you were sufficiently mature to attend a party without my constant supervision. No, don't try to make excuses. Bob told me you were out here drinking beer, and it's not at all surprising that the juvenile delinquents should have gravitated to you."

The tirade went on and on as Jane gripped Amy's arm and propelled her from the room. Patrick was appalled, but he saw no reasonable way that he could intercede. Jane could probably knock him down even more handily than Bruce. Amy seemed to grow visibly smaller and paler and more mouse-like, shrinking into herself as they left.

He followed them through the Hall to see them into their coats and out the door, but Jane was too busy scolding her daughter to spare him more than the curtest goodnight. And Amy seemed ashamed even to look at him.

The departure of the Miniters seemed to signal the end of the party, but Patrick supposed that was coincidental. The food and drink ran out at about the same time. As he guided the last of the guests to the door, he saw Rose striding briskly toward the kitchen, and he felt some relief. The situation upstairs, whatever it was, seemed to have resolved itself.

Some neighbors — Jane Miniter, principally, who sold real estate and therefore had a vested interest in promoting the myth of bucolic tranquility — often expressed amusement at the number and variety of locks on the front door of the mill, and Patrick was usually inclined to agree, but tonight it reassured him to lock the door thoroughly before turning back into the suddenly empty and quiet house.

He checked the ground-floor rooms for burning cigarettes and passed-out guests, securing doors and windows. Drained of humanity, the Great Hall looked squalid. The bare skeleton of the turkey reigned over a clutter of soiled paper plates and plastic glasses and overflowing ashtrays. Frank's lurking figures had lost all semblance of malefic life. They were only old clothes and plaster. A dull glow of dawn paled the surviving candles. The music had ended, so he dug out one of Rose's old vinyl discs and cued *The Entrance of the Gods into Valhalla.*

Something was wrong. Those ringing hammers — they belonged in another part of Wagner's *Ring.* He realized that the sound was coming from somewhere else within the mill, and that he had been hearing it for some time without registering it.

In the kitchen, the noise was louder. Some metal object might have been caught in the framework of the absent mill-wheel and was being knocked against the wall by the current. But when he opened the back door to check this theory, the sound was inaudible above the noise of the stream. The sound must be coming from inside the house. He paused to draw a few lungfuls of damp, smokeless air before closing the door and locking it.

When he turned back to the kitchen, he noticed that the door to the cellar stood open.

He tried to convince himself that some defect in the furnace was responsible for the noise, but he couldn't believe it. He knew what was causing the rhythmic, clinking, hammering noise.

He walked to the head of the stairs. The only light down there came from the section fronting the pond, as it had done the other day, but now it was stronger.

"Rose?" he called. "Mom!"

The hammering continued. It was quite loud now. Unmistakably, it was the ring of a spike or a chisel being driven into stone.

He was still afraid of the cellar, but that fear was swept away by worse ones. If Rose succeeded in breaking through the foundation of the building, she might be drowned. Whether she succeeded or not, her action suggested a seriously disordered state of mind. He ran down the stairs.

The dim bulb hanging from the ceiling had been augmented by the orange glow of a kerosene lamp at Rose's feet. Gripping a sledge-hammer in bleeding hands, she swung against the wall from her waist with the rhythmic, tireless strokes of a clockwork figure.

"Rose!" he shouted, running to her. She must have heard him, for she swung the hammer with redoubled force.

Her face with its chalky makeup wore a look of trancelike concentration. He was forced to jump to avoid her backswing when he came closer. The impact of the hammer against the chisel spattered her blood on him. He hung back, timing her strokes, then rushed in to seize her. He tried to avoid using force and smother her freedom of movement with his greater size, but that proved impossible. She fought back violently, ramming the haft of the hammer against his chest and arms.

While he squirmed to avoid knees aimed at his groin, she spewed out a torrent of meaningless words in a detached monotone: ". . . father you bastard can't steal my birthright I'm the daughter of God you queer let me get through that wall and claim it oh let me Mordred promised me —"

She kept gibbering such nonsense as she flung herself from side to side and tried to get a clean swing at him with the hammer. He had abandoned his scruples about using force, and she just wasn't strong enough to break his grip. His only hope seemed to be to exhaust her to the point where he could lead or carry her upstairs. Then he might tie her to her bed and call a doctor.

"Mom — Mother, please calm down, please! I'm not trying to hurt you. It's late. Let's go upstairs, what do you say?"

"Fuck me you bastard father, yes yes!" she grunted, and she began to twist and squirm in a different way, a way that was even scarier. "Fuck me, Father, yes, fuck me!"

The hammer clanged and clattered to the floor. She ripped her dress open down the front and rubbed his thigh vigorously with her pubic-mound as she alternately kissed and bit his face. He thrust her away from him in horror and self-loathing. She snatched up the sledge and rushed at him, jerking it back over her shoulder in preparation for a murderous blow.

He hit her on the chin with even more force than he had used against Bruce Curtis. She staggered back, then fell against the wall and slid to a heap on the floor. Sobbing apologies, he fell to his knees beside her. She was out cold, but he determined that she was breathing regularly and her pulse was strong.

His concern for her lost its overriding urgency in the next instant as a section of the wall, the very section that she had claimed was a door, swung inward to reveal a flight of stairs descending into darkness.

Chapter Eight

*F*rank was suspicious of his euphoric mood, but not even the most vigorous self-analysis could dispel it. *Disaster* was a word pitifully inadequate to describe the Hallowe'en party. Disaster had stumbled upon the heels of disaster. Any one of them, taken by itself, might have driven a lesser man to suicide. Yet here he stood at his easel, swept up in a creative frenzy and all but laughing out of sheer high spirits and self-satisfaction as he worked.

The work was difficult, perhaps the most difficult he had ever undertaken, but he felt eminently capable of doing it. He had spent almost all of Sunday trying every conceivable combination of his Winsor Newton oils before he had hit upon a simple blend of burnt umber with cadmium orange to create the precise shade of her dark-red hair. The certainty that he had achieved perfection in this one small thing was enough reason for euphoria.

Balanced against that little triumph was the fact that he had lost his most important magazine connection, and perhaps a few others. It didn't seem to matter very much. He had wasted far too much of his life on commercial hackwork anyway. It was long past time that he did something he wanted to do — something he urgently needed to do. Losing Roberts had most likely been a blessing in disguise, a much-needed kick out of a comfortable rut.

Thinking about Roberts came close to souring his mood, but not even the memory of that disgusting incident could fully quell his high spirits. Trying hard to remember the details, his attitude was more accurately one of bewilderment than disgust. He couldn't remember having drunk all that much, but he must have drunk himself into a truly psychotic state in order to confuse a voluptuous young woman with that creature. Even in bed he had been deceived, although the details of their dalliance were mercifully dim. He did recall that he'd actually been screwing him when the lights crashed on and he came to his senses. No, he couldn't say that he'd come to his senses, not even then, because he'd reacted by trying to bash poor Roberts into a pulp. The final irony was added when Howard Ashcroft, who had been asked to the party only for his value as a loony conversation-piece, had restrained him and talked him back to a semblance of rationality.

And Patrick — what kind of evil vibrations had been charging the air that night? It was reprehensible that he should have hit Roberts; it was an uncharacteristic reaction and, all things considered, an unfair one; however, in his younger days, he had struck other men. But as far as he knew, Patrick had never hit anybody in his life. He would have been willing to bet that he was incapable of it. Yet he had not only hit somebody, he had put him in the hospital in a coma. He had learned of that this morning, when somebody named Curtis had called and babbled about a lawsuit against him and his brutal monster of a son.

The greatest disaster, of course, had befallen Rose. She had been sedated to a zombie for the past twenty-four hours. Dr. Keller, a tottering old fuddy-duddy who still made house-calls, had clearly been trying to prepare him for the worst: she would have to be sent to a hospital. He had hinted at the rediscovered virtues of electroshock therapy, which he himself had never stopped believing in.

He supposed it all could have been worse. No stranger but Howard Ashcroft had witnessed his own mortification, and he doubted that Ashcroft was the sort of person to spread the story around town. And everyone had left before Rose had staged her scene.

He could even cite some good that had come out of the mess. Rose — it was a harsh judgment, but he felt it was true — had been verging on a mental breakdown for a long time. Now that she had finally slipped all the way over the edge, she would get the help she needed. Best of all, her outburst had uncovered a library of ancient books and papers beneath the cellar. They might prove to be valuable. They had damned well better be, what with the lawsuits and doctor-bills about to pile up at his door.

"Oh, shit!" He put his brush down and reached for a cigarette.

While his mind had wandered, he had inadvertently altered the balance of his composition. The full-length portrait had a somber, murky background. That had been his intention, but he had just made one of the shadows a little too dark. It suggested a second figure skulking behind the black-gowned woman. He was still wondering how to deal with this alteration in his original concept when the front doorbell rang.

He ignored it, as usual. Rose would get it. When it kept on ringing, he felt a twinge of irritation toward her. Didn't she realize — no, of course she didn't. He hurried downstairs, hoping to reach the door before the noise penetrated her sedation.

"Why, uh —" It took him a moment to recognize the impeccably dressed, silver-haired man at the door as George Spencer, Rupert's father. He was a lawyer, and Frank's greeting was less than expansive: "George.

Hello."

"Frank, how are you?"

He felt that the words conveyed more than a trite greeting, but maybe he was being paranoid. When he said nothing, George continued: "May I come in and have a word with you?"

"Sure, come in. What is it, this Curtis — is that the name, Curtis? This Curtis thing?"

"I'm sorry. I don't understand."

"Oh. Well, that's good. I thought you might be here in some kind of legal capacity. Somebody says he's going to sue us over an incident at the party. Come in, come in. I hope they also remember to send us the guns and money."

He doubted that George got the allusion to the Warren Zevon song, but he smiled politely. He seemed vaguely reluctant to enter. Perhaps he was put off by Frank's working clothes. George wore a three-piece lawyer-suit with a velvet-collared topcoat and gray homburg. Frank knew that he himself was dressed as if he had just broken into the house after spending the night in an alley. He reflected that he didn't know him very well. The mill was Rose's inheritance, and he had gladly let her handle all those legalities with George.

"I don't know about any litigation," George said, finally entering and closing the door behind himself. "What. . . ?"

"Patrick got into a fight with another kid, and now his parents are claiming that he suffered a serious injury. I didn't even know about it at the time. It doesn't sound like Patrick, does it?"

George mumbled provisional agreement while Frank moved toward the liquor cabinet. He hadn't planned to start drinking until he'd done more work, but he suspected that he would soon need a drink. He interpreted the lawyer's nervousness as a preamble to the revelation of some brand new disaster connected with Saturday night.

"What will you have?" Frank asked as he pulled out the vodka.

"Well, it's a little early — no, on second thought, I'll have a scotch and water, if that's convenient. Mostly water, please."

Frank went to the kitchen for ice, thankful for the brief reprieve. It gave him time to reflect that George probably wouldn't have accepted a drink if he'd come here to complain of some atrocity. He reviewed in his mind his contact with the Spencers that night. As far as he could remember, he'd done nothing to offend them, but God only knew what Patrick or Rose had done. He remembered Madge's — or was it Marge? — inane comment about the scene reminding her of *The Masque of the Red Death.* She didn't know how right she'd been.

"Sit down, George, please," Frank said, returning. "Take off your coat and tell me what's wrong."

"It shows, does it? Bad habit for a lawyer to get into. But — well, I am upset, Frank. Maybe I'm worrying unnecessarily. It's nothing that I can put my finger on exactly."

Frank settled in an easy chair, satisfied that George's complaint, whatever it was, couldn't be as dire as the things he already knew about. Maybe he was worried about Rupert's crush on Rose. That seemed an odd concern for the father of a grown man nowadays, but perhaps George saw himself as an old-school Yankee patriarch who held lifelong authority over his offspring. He hoped he could keep a straight face when George asked him if Rose's intentions were honorable.

"It's about Patrick," George said.

"Yes?" Frank tried to conceal his annoyance at being proved wrong so quickly.

"I had a most unusual interview with him this morning."

George obviously wasn't a person out of whom news bubbled. Frank considered the statement for a moment, then said: "I thought he was in school."

George nodded. "That in itself was one of the minor anomalies of the interview."

Frank took a hefty gulp of vodka. He was struck by a ludicrous fancy: George Spencer, deliberate and sensitive to precise shades of meaning, cross-examining the scatterbrained Mrs. Minotaur in a murder-trial. It would be the Trial of the Century, in that it just might take that long.

"Please go on," Frank said, fighting unseemly laughter.

"As I said, it's difficult to put my finger on the exact cause of my concern. I can only say that Patrick seemed much changed from the young person I thought I knew."

"Why did he see you? To consult you about that Curtis — ?"

"No, no, he didn't mention that. He came for a purpose quite unrelated. I wonder if I might interject a query about Rose's health."

Frank was sorely tempted to play his game with him and answer, "Of course you might," but he suspected that George would find nothing unusual in that response. He said, "She's not at all well. She's suffered a sort of nervous breakdown."

George nodded. "That's what I derived from Patrick. I asked him, routinely, how his mother was, and he replied — I believe this is an exact quote — 'She remains humorous.'"

"Huh?"

"My reaction exactly!" Perhaps George strictly rationed his smiles because he knew they appeared sly, shark-like: they didn't inspire confidence. "I was quite baffled. When I asked him to explain himself, he said — again, I am reasonably certain that these are his exact words — 'I meant to say that her humors are yet in violent contention.'"

"Which is a sixteenth-century way of saying that somebody is nuts."

George seemed pained by Frank's bluntness. "Precisely. During the course of our conversation, he chose several times to express himself in a fancifully archaic way."

"Well, 'fanciful' is the operative word there. He's always been that. I noticed him speaking like a Jacobean tragedy a couple of times during the party. He was just slipping into a role, that's all, and he hasn't slipped out of it yet. I used to talk like John Wayne for a week after I'd seen one of his movies. That's all it is."

"Perhaps." George remained obviously unconvinced. "I would submit, however, that this quirk, taken together with his unaccustomed truancy and the incident at the party, constitute an odd pattern of behavior."

"Christ, George, I'm not the goddamn Supreme Court! Why don't you just come right out and say what's on your mind?"

George was unruffled by his outburst. He said with a shrug, "I wish I could, but it's all so . . . tenuous. What I'm suggesting, I suppose, is that Patrick's concern for his mother may have upset his own mental balance, and that he might need psychiatric help as badly as she does. I'm sorry to put it so baldly —"

"No, not at all. I suppose it's something I might not notice, being close to him, especially at a time like this, when Rose is my main concern. But what did he come to see you about in the first place? He didn't just wander in off the street to spout Elizabethan lingo at you, did he?"

"I almost forgot, even though it tends to support my thesis." He paused to ponder for a moment.

Frank found that his glass was empty, while George had barely touched his drink. He refused to be deterred by the lawyer's sterling example. He got up and poured himself another.

"He said," George continued, "that he'd found some papers in the cellar relating to one of his ancestors. The papers made reference to one Mirdath Hodgson, a daughter of his ancestor. He asked me if I knew anything about this person; specifically, if I knew where she might be buried."

"Were you able to tell him?"

"No. I have made a special study of local history, but I can't account for every person who might have lived here in 1847." George's tone suggested vexation with some multitude who supposed that he could. "I directed him to the church records, and he laughed — rather unpleasantly, if I may say so. But as I said, he didn't seem at all like himself."

"Well, he did find some papers in the cellar, you know."

George appeared startled. "He did? I thought. . . ."

"You thought that was part of his delusion, huh? No, the papers are quite real, although I haven't examined them."

"That would be . . . extraordinary. You see, Patrick's ancestor, a man named Mordred Glendower, had an unwholesome reputation. When Patrick began affecting his archaic mannerisms, I believed he might be living out a fantasy of identifying with that person. And maybe that is exactly what he is doing. The discovery of the papers gives him an understandable excuse. I feel somewhat relieved."

"Wait a minute. When I said *Jacobean,* I wasn't referring to James K. Polk."

George actually laughed. His laugh, a high-pitched cackle, was even less infectious than his smile. "According to local legend, Mordred was born in 1560, in the reign of Elizabeth, actually."

"By the time I'm two hundred and eighty-seven, I suppose I will have acquired an unwholesome reputation, too."

"Mordred was believed to have found the secret of eternal life through the practice of loathsome rituals that included eating the flesh of infants." George leaned forward in his chair, displaying surprising enthusiasm for his subject. "There was also gossip about an incestuous liaison with that daughter. It was believed that he could pass on his powers only to someone entirely of his own descent — that is, to a child by his own daughter." He stopped short, suddenly disconcerted, as if remembering too late that he was talking about an ancestor of Frank's wife and son. He added lamely, "All nonsense, of course."

"No, please, go on. Don't worry about sparing my feelings. Nonsense or not, it's all water under the bridge."

"There isn't much more to tell. Not that I know of, at any rate. People became outraged at Mordred's alleged crimes and burned his house down around his ears. Naturally, he became a local legend after that, with his ghost lurking around the mill or stealing children from nearby farms." With a shark-smile probably intended to be playful, he added: "You haven't seen any ghosts, have you?"

"Not sober." Frank got up and moved to the cabinet, noting with annoyance that George's glass was still nearly full. "And the daughter? Did she die in the fire, too?"

"According to one version, she did. A more common variant holds that she escaped the fire by rendering herself invisible, but that she was later caught and hanged. We might find out something by examining the papers that Patrick mentioned. Would you let me see them?"

"You've made me quite curious myself. Come along."

Leading the way to the cellar, it occurred to Frank that he shouldn't have been so forthcoming in allowing George to view the skeletons in the Glenn family closet. Perhaps Rose and Patrick really were descended from a homicidal maniac and his daughter, and perhaps some proof of that had been locked in the cellar. His hesitation was only momentary. George was the closest thing they had to a family lawyer, and he was discreet to a fault. Anyway, the supposed crimes had been committed a long time ago. Nobody whose opinion was worth notice would hold them against his wife and son.

He winced with sudden guilt. Patrick had spent all of yesterday buried in the cellar with the hidden library, not even emerging for meals. Preoccupied with Rose's problems and his own work, Frank had hardly noticed, nor had he even bothered to ask Patrick what his research had uncovered. Today Patrick was acting weirdly, as George had reported. There could easily be a direct connection. Evidence of a heritage of murder and incest might have unhinged him.

The door of the secret room still stood open. Frank snapped on the flashlight he had taken from the kitchen and led the way down into a large room lined from floor to ceiling with books. He lit the two candles that stood on a table in the center, which was littered with parchment scrolls and mouldy volumes.

"This is odd, isn't?" Frank said. "These books — Latin, Greek, French, German, and here's a language I don't even recognize — they aren't the sort of thing you'd expect to find in a miller's library."

"The mill would have been a cover for his true occupation. After all, three-hundred-year-old wizards don't hang out shingles to advertise their services."

He glanced sharply at George, who had donned rimless glasses to examine the books on the table, but he couldn't determine if he was being facetious. "Are you suggesting that he really was one?"

"No, merely that he really believed he was, and that his neighbors did. It would explain why he felt obliged to conceal his library like this."

Frank nodded as he toured the room and made a casual inventory. Rose's ancestor had backed up his delusions with profound scholarship. He took down some of the books and inspected the title pages with the aid of his flashlight: *De Artibus Magicis,* Cologne, 1482; *De Maleficiis,* of Arnauld de Villeneuve, Lyons, 1509; *Stratagemata Satanae* — in ten volumes — of Acontius, printed in Basle in 1565; William Godwin's *Lives of the Necromancers,* London, 1834; *Unaussprechlichen Kulten* of Von Junzt, printed in 1839 in Düsseldorf; Boulton's *Compleat Historie of Magick, Sorcery and Witchcraft,* London, 1715.

George's voice was oddly strained as he said: "You know, this library and its contents might constitute the most elaborate hoax since the Piltdown Man."

Frank turned from the shelves he had been browsing and saw that George was leafing through a large, leather-bound volume with iron clasps. His expression in the flickering candlelight shifted from disbelief to exasperation to wry amusement.

"What makes you say that? What sort of a hoax?"

George peered at him over his glasses for a moment before he asked, "Have you ever heard of a writer named H.P. Lovecraft?"

"No. Should I have?"

"Perhaps not." George set the heavy book on the table and leaned down to examine it, page by page, as he spoke. "During his life he was possibly the world's most obscure and neglected author, selling his stories — horror stories — to pulp magazines for a pittance or even giving them away for nothing to amateur publications. He died of cancer and malnutrition in 1937. Some years after his death his work enjoyed a considerable vogue, selling millions of copies in paperback — too late to help poor Lovecraft, of course."

"And that's one of his books?"

"In a way, it is." George laughed nervously. "At least, I always thought it was his creation."

"I don't understand."

"Lovecraft was no mere writer of ghost stories. He invented an elaborate mythology on which he based his tales. It involved the expulsion from our world in prehistoric times of certain alien entities — the Great Old Ones, he called them — who still lurk at the fringes of our space-time continuum, waiting for their chance to return and take over."

Frank tried not to smile. His perception of George Spencer as a level-headed realist — wounded when George had told the juicy story of Mordred Glendower with such evident relish — had just suffered a fatal blow. Not only was he an enthusiastic collector of old scandals, he was apparently also an expert on pulp-magazine horror stories.

"This is a bit confusing. This room has presumably been sealed since eighteen-forty-something, but if Lovecraft died ninety years after that —"

"That's what I'm coming to. I said that the mythology he created was elaborate. It included the invention of a complete bibliography of his Great Old Ones. One of his favorite tricks was to cite a list of books you might find in any good library — the *Malleus Maleficarum*, for instance, or Cotton Mather's *Wonders of the Invisible World*, or Ludvig Prinn's *Mysteries of the Worm*, or Frazer's *Golden Bough* — and stick one of his imaginary titles in with them. It lent great verisimilitude to his stories. So much so, in fact, that many people — myself included, I must admit — have gone on wild-goose chases in libraries and antique bookstores, looking for Lovecraft's mythical titles."

George seemed embarrassed by that admission of folly, and he fell silent as he continued to study the book before him.

"And?"

"The most important of these non-existent books, the work central to Lovecraft's mythology, was called the *Necronomicon*, by Abdul Alhazred. It was supposed to be a book of spells and incantations that could, quite literally, raise hell. Lovecraft tells us that the copies in Widener Library and the British Museum were closely guarded under lock and key to keep them from falling into the wrong hands."

"I think I see what it is you find so difficult to come out and tell me." Frank returned to the table and laid his hand on the book. "That this book —"

"That this book is the *Necronomicon*," George said, his voice breaking into high-pitched laughter, "rendered into English by Dr. John Dee and printed in London in 1589."

Frank saw that the title page was just as George had described it. He turned the mouldering pages until he met with a shock: a postcard depicting the charms of Mystic Seaport. It took him a moment to realize that Patrick must have used the card to mark his place. A contemptuous smile touched his lips as he read aloud a passage on the indicated page:

"'Call not upon *Yog-Sothoth* until ye be certaine that ye Bones be compleat and culled of forraine contamination. For it hath been known in antient Tymes that ye Bones of a Man mingled with ye Bones of a Beare or a Lyon, or even with ye Offaille of a lowly Coney or Porpentine, hath produced for a hapless Necromancer not a Resurrection of that which was, but a Creation of Abomination that should not be.'

"Well," Frank said, "obviously Lovecraft didn't invent the book."

"Damn it, Frank, there is no such book!" George cried, thumping it with his fist. "I told you, I was half-convinced by the deadpan realism of his stories. I actually looked for the *Necronomicon* whenever I happened to be near those libraries — the Widener at Harvard, the British Museum, the Bibliothèque Nationale. I asked the experts in such places if they'd ever heard of it. They said they hadn't — although some had heard of Lovecraft and got a laugh out of my questions."

"Possibly they thought yours were the wrong hands for it to fall into." He was annoyed that George had felt it necessary to tell him where Widener was, even if he was wearing his Syracuse sweatshirt.

George ignored the jibe. "This Dr. Dee was a real person, though, a scholar and astrologer with a somewhat shady reputation. But nowhere is he credited — except by Lovecraft, and of course on this title-page — with translating such a work."

Frank returned to his examination of the disputed volume. It was in extremely poor condition, as smudged and stained and dog-eared as a favorite cookbook. Some of the pages had been torn and crudely mended; others were mutilated or missing entirely. Worms and mould and dampness had worked their mischief, too. The book could have been forged, but it was hard to believe that the damage could have been so effectively simulated. It seemed the genuine result of centuries of hard use.

"If it's a hoax," Frank said, "it means that somebody went to the trouble of writing this thing — all six hundred double-column pages of it — printing it on antique vellum in sixteenth-century typography and giving it four hundred years of artificial aging. They then assembled a whole library of old and presumably valuable volumes around it, about a thousand in all — and are they *all* forgeries? — and squirreled them away in a secret room in an abandoned mill, a place where they might never be discovered. Who do you suppose is behind the hoax, Bill Gates? I can't think of anybody else with enough money to pull it off. And why play a trick like this on the Laughlins? I never heard of Lovecraft or the *Nickelodeon,* and I doubt that Rose or Patrick has, either."

George displayed no appreciation at all of his wit. He seemed to have aged ten years in the past few minutes. His skin looked gray. "You've convinced me," he said, his voice shaky. "But if it's not a hoax. . . ."

"Sit down," Frank said, drawing out the only chair and pushing him down gently but firmly. "You don't look at all well."

"I don't feel well, Frank. If this damned book is real —"

"It only means that Lovecraft knew more about rare books than people gave him credit for, and that there are a lot of ill-informed librarians in the world, that's all. It doesn't mean that Lovecraft's stories are factual, or that whatever nonsense this book might contain is the truth. I have a real copy of the Bible upstairs; does that mean it's all true? You're an attorney, George. Do you think that any of this constitutes a *prima facie* case for the existence of your Great Old Ones?"

George at last managed a smile. "You're right, of course. It's just that Lovecraft exerted quite a grip on my imagination when I was an impressionable teen-ager. Finding this book — well, how would you feel, skeptic though you are, if a suave European nobleman named Dracula moved in next door to you and you noticed that your neck had acquired a couple of puncture-wounds?"

"I'd feel like moving, which is what I think we should both do. Let's go upstairs and get some air."

They returned to the living room, where George refused another drink as he collected his topcoat and hat.

"I'd like to ask you a great favor," he said.

That approach to a request invariably set Frank's teeth on edge. "You can certainly ask," he said.

"Keep Patrick away from these books. From a purely practical standpoint, he's overwrought, and nothing down there could improve his state of mind."

"I think that's not your real reason for asking, though."

"No, but I think that you'll agree it's a sensible one. Some people — Colin Wilson in England, Christophe Thill in France, S.T. Joshi in this country, for instance — have made serious studies of Lovecraft and his sources. I'm going to try to get in touch with them this afternoon and see if I can determine the truth about that book."

"All right, scratch Bill Gates. The hoax was obviously perpetrated by the phone company to run up your bill."

He succeeded in getting one of George's unpleasant laughs, but he suspected that the lawyer was merely trying to be polite.

Chapter Nine

*R*ain began to fall as Rupert Spencer turned into the winding drive that led to the mill. His windshield-wipers had succeeded only in spreading a film of road grime in front of his eyes when he came upon a girl standing squarely in his way. He hit the brakes and the horn at the same time and felt his rear wheels begin to slide on the wet gravel. He swerved onto the lawn, where the car came to a bumpy halt.

He lowered the window and glared at her, but she wasn't even looking toward him. She continued to stand in the center of the drive, at the point where it began to widen into a parking area. All her attention was fixed on the mill.

Rupert rejected the first harsh words that came to his lips, but his tone of voice conveyed his irritation as he said, "You're getting wet."

A moment passed before she turned to look at him, and her glance merely acknowledged his existence. Then she returned her attention to the mill. He was forced to follow the direction of her stare, but he saw only the blank face of the hulking building. The light was rapidly draining from the day as the sun set somewhere unnoticed behind the clouds, but no lights showed in the windows.

"For Christ's sake," he muttered, annoyed with himself for having been drawn into sharing her obsession, for having expected to see something extraordinary.

He jerked up the collar of his trenchcoat and got out of the car. He walked up beside her. She was perhaps fifteen or sixteen years old and very pretty. She cradled a load of schoolbooks in front of her ample breasts, clearly outlined by her wet blouse.

"Your books are getting wet, too," he said gruffly. "Why don't you go inside?"

"I can't. He hasn't asked me."

"Who?"

"Patrick."

Her attention was so intently focused on the mill that he was compelled to make a second and more detailed survey from her point of view. The timbers were darkened by rain. Sheets of water sluiced down the skylight of Frank's studio. He could see no one at any of the black windows.

"Tell you what, I'll ask you to sit in my car. At least you won't get any wetter."

She again turned her vacant blue eyes toward him. He didn't believe that she was mentally deficient, but her mind was obviously somewhere else at the moment. She allowed herself to be drawn along when he plucked at the sleeve of her white, oversized school sweater. He opened the door on the passenger's side for her, then sprinted back to his own door with his shoulders hunched against the rain. He raised the window and adjusted the heater to maximum output. She seemed neither more nor less content to sit in the car and gaze at the house than she had been to stand in the rain and gaze at it.

"My name's Rupert Spencer, by the way." After a long silence, he added, "What's yours?"

"Shana Jennings."

"You're a friend of Patrick's?"

"Yes."

He found it hard to believe that a girl this attractive would even notice Patrick, much less mope around his house in the pouring rain in hope of seeing him, but that was apparently the case. Her manner suggested someone nearly deranged by hopeless love.

"I came to see his mother." Rupert reflected bitterly that there was a lot of that — derangement by hopeless love — going around lately. "I'm told she's ill. Won't you come inside with me and —"

"I couldn't."

"Why not?"

"Patrick told me to come here and wait for him."

"I see," he said, although he was more puzzled than ever. His curiosity about the strange girl and her relation to Patrick was no more than mild, but he indulged it to postpone what would probably be an unpleasant encounter with Frank. To keep her talking, he said, "I heard that Patrick's taking his mother's illness pretty hard, that he's acting oddly. Have you noticed anything unusual about him lately?"

"No." He was startled when she turned to show him a face that would have made a dying pilgrim at Lourdes seem blasé and added, "The only thing I notice lately is how wonderful he is. I could kill myself! He's the most wonderful person who ever lived, and I never knew it before. When I think of how I disrespected him. . . . I love him, I want to do everything for him, only I'm not worthy of him. I feel like a worm in love with the sun. Or like a slug, something under a rock that the sun wouldn't even want to know about."

"Don't sell yourself short," he said uneasily, embarrassed by her passionate outburst. He doubted that she even heard him as she returned her enraptured gaze to the house.

He wondered if the girl's behavior was related to the situation at the Laughlins', as sketched by his father. Perhaps they were all victims of some contagious hysteria. He decided he didn't have enough data to make a judgement. Extracting information from George was usually difficult, but the difficulty was infinitely compounded when the information concerned Rose Laughlin. Nothing had ever been openly spoken on the subject, but he sensed that his father knew he was in love with her and thoroughly disapproved.

All he had been told was that Rose had suffered a nervous collapse, that Patrick was acting oddly, and that Frank, although expressing concern for them, seemed to be in an inappropriate mood of manic effervescence. Perhaps Shana provided the simple reason for Patrick's behavior. He might act oddly, too, if he were a shy misfit who suddenly became the object of a prototypical prom queen's all-consuming passion. Nor was her own behavior all that strange, though extreme: people were always falling in love with unlikely people.

As they always did, his thoughts returned to Rose. A woman like her married to a buffoon like Frank had every reason in the world to suffer a nervous breakdown, but he couldn't shake the thought that her breakdown had come at a time suspiciously advantageous to her husband. She had spoken of a treasure buried in the cellar; she had apparently found it; and now her husband maintained that she had gone crazy.

He found it hard to credit the most sinister interpretation. Despite his dislike of Frank, he didn't believe that he was capable of railroading his wife into a madhouse in order to swindle her. He might be crude and selfish, but he wasn't actively villainous. An argument in his favor was the nature of the "treasure" itself, as his father had described it, a cache of old books and papers that had been stashed in a damp cellar for more than a century.

Nevertheless he had to see Rose, to find out for himself whether her husband was telling the truth about her condition. More important than that, he had to beg her forgiveness. She had asked him a favor, the first favor she had ever asked of him that would have caused him any inconvenience, and he had turned her down. It was particularly painful to consider because, in moments of romantic self-indulgence, he thought of his place in her life as that of a pledged knight in the days of courtly love. When a dragon had actually appeared, he had turned his back and forced her to face it herself. Her breakdown had coincided with her discovery in the cellar. If he had been with her, or if he had gone alone, she might have been spared whatever shock had precipitated her illness.

Still he hesitated, staring at the house like Shana. He felt a certain kinship with her. They were both infatuated: in the true sense of the word, made foolish. He was on a fool's errand, as Frank would surely tell him. But he had to see her.

He was still trying to muster the courage needed to go and ring the doorbell when a tap at his window jolted him. He jerked around to see Patrick grinning down at him. He rolled down the window, somewhat relieved. If Patrick admitted him to the house, he might not even need to see Frank.

"I came to see Rose. I heard that —"

"She will no doubt be delighted to receive you, Master Rupert," Patrick said, his grin escalating to a toothy grimace. "I have many pressing matters to attend to, but you must know the way to her bed-chamber."

Rupert wondered how to take that. It could have been an innocent remark, but the crazy grin on Patrick's face left it open to salacious interpretation. Perhaps this was an example of what George had termed his odd behavior. He certainly looked odd, with his hair hanging lank and wet around his bony face, and one of his eyes seemed unable to focus, staring off to one side while he fixed Rupert with the other. Patrick was not wearing his glasses, perhaps because of the rain, and that might have explained the defect.

While they spoke, Shana slipped out of the car to stand beside Patrick, gazing up at him with the dumb adoration of a dog for its master. She trembled, and Rupert suspected it was less a reaction to the rain and the cold than to Patrick's presence.

"You have met Mistress Jennings?" Patrick casually squeezed one of her breasts. The gesture shocked Rupert: not just because the normally shy youth was doing it, but because it seemed neither sexual nor affectionate, but coldly proprietary.

"Yes, and don't you think you should take her inside?" It irritated him to speak of her as he would of a dog, but that was the role she had chosen. "She's soaked."

"Of course. Come along, dear heart, we'll soon rid you of your wet garments." Patrick's little laugh was chilling.

He followed them into the house, noting that Patrick carried a large book. He wondered if that was part of the cache from the cellar, and what the rain would do to its value. A closer look revealed that it was some kind of ledger, and its worn but rugged binding suggested an institutional origin. His father had told him that Patrick was seeking burial records.

"Looks like you've been looting the Town Hall," he observed as they entered the house, which was darker and seemed nearly as damp as the outside.

Patrick turned and fixed him with a stare that was alarming in its intensity. Rupert found himself taking an involuntary step backward. Then Patrick's crazy grin reappeared.

"You need not trouble yourself with my affairs. You'll find my lady mother in her chamber."

With that he turned and gave Shana a shove that sent her stumbling through the living room, leaving Rupert to close the front door. He removed his coat and took his time brushing the rain from it before hanging it on the rack by the door, still delaying the moment when he would have to face Rose.

He felt sorry for the girl. Patrick had always seemed an essentially kind person, considerate of others' feelings, despite a certain cold reserve that he had attributed to shyness; but Shana's blind devotion had apparently brought out a thoroughly unpleasant side of his nature. In that regard, perhaps he took after Frank.

He walked through the Great Hall, noting that nobody had bothered to clean up after the party or remove the decorations. Frank's funhouse sculptures still menaced from dark corners. One of them, a tall, thin figure in black whose flesh had partly peeled from the bone, didn't invite close inspection.

He mounted the stairs quietly and turned down the hall on the second floor. Contrary to Patrick's snide assertion, he didn't know which door led to Rose's bedroom, but a light showed under a door at the end of the hall. He knocked.

There was no response. He knocked again, then turned the knob and entered. It was a huge room at the rear of the house. One wall was a window facing the depressing prospect of the rain-swept pond. Rose, sitting in bed with her back toward him, gazed out that window.

"Rose?" he said softly.

"Rupert, what a pleasant surprise!"

She looked normal, though pale. Asked to pick the crazy one by looks alone, he would surely have opted for Patrick. He breathed, and the act made him aware that he had been neglecting it for the past minute or so.

"How are you?" He advanced warily.

"Exhausted, but I think that's due to the damned pills they've been pushing on me. I only pretended to take them today. What's going on around here?"

He sat gingerly on the edge of the bed. For a moment he could only gaze at her. He had prepared himself for every eventuality except the sudden desire that he now felt, and it embarrassed him. He remembered vividly how warm and soft her lips were, how naturally her body had fit against his on the one occasion they had kissed. She looked vulnerable and appealing in her white robe, with her black hair unbound around her shoulders.

He cleared his throat. "I'm not sure what's going on. That's why I came, to find out."

She smiled wryly and looked down at her hands. The fingers were long and bony, the palms broad and competent. A less interested observer would have said they were not pretty hands, and they revealed her age more clearly than anything else, but he had always loved them. Now her palms were bandaged. He thought it best not to ask why. It took an effort not to seize her injured hands and kiss them.

"I can't tell you anything," she said with a laugh. "I don't even know what day it is."

"Monday. They seem to think you're. . . ."

"Yeah, crazy, I know that. I drank a lot at the party after you left, far too much. I began to —" she hesitated — "to see things. But Dr. Ashcroft calmed me down. I had no idea that he'd turn out to be such a nice man. But then they always depict the Devil himself as a charming gentleman, don't they? Pardon me if I'm babbling, but what's the point of being crazy if you can't babble? No, Rupert, don't look so stricken, I'm only making a bad joke. Anyway, I was talking quite rationally to Howard, I could even play back the conversation up to a point, but at that point I apparently blacked out. The next thing I remember I was lying here in bed, chattering away at Dr. Keller. I couldn't seem to stop. So he started pushing those pills on me, and that wiped me out until about noon today, when I decided that I didn't want to spend the rest of my life unconscious. Frank pops in every once in a while to feed me another pill, and I hide it under my tongue while I drink the water. Then I spit it out when he's gone."

She laughed merrily. He was far from amused, but he made himself smile.

"Do you want me to get you out of here?"

"What on earth for? I live here."

He avoided her eyes. "Frank thinks that you need a psychiatrist, but I can't see it. If you want my opinion, your only problem is Frank. Once you get away from him —"

"You're sweet, Rupert, you really are, but isn't this the same dumb conversation we had on Saturday night?"

Gazing into her eyes made him dizzy. "There was one significant difference," he said, and he leaned forward to kiss her.

That first time she had merely accepted his kiss, but now she responded to it. Her mouth opened, her tongue sought his. His hand slid inside her robe to fondle her bare breast. She arched her back, pushing her breast into firmer contact with his hand.

He retreated in confusion, because the next moves seemed otherwise inevitable. He wanted her desperately, but no time or place could have been worse. This was Frank's bed, too, and he might walk in at any moment. Even though she seemed perfectly rational, he couldn't deny the possibility that he might be taking advantage of her illness.

"Why did you stop?"

"For Christ's sake, Rose!" He got up and stalked to the window, running stiff, nervous fingers through his hair. "Anybody could walk in on us."

"Well, you could always lock the door."

He turned to face her. Whatever words he meant to speak on the subject of propriety were lost forever as he saw that she had shed her robe and the bedclothes. Her trim thighs moved to a slow and sensuous inner rhythm as she lay before him and stared up into his eyes with unashamed desire.

Unexpectedly, he found the strength to turn his back on her. "Rose, I'm not going to make love to you in your husband's bed. I want you to come away with me. I want to make love to you, but I want a lot more than that. I want to be with you forever."

"Rupert, you're such a dope. Frank doesn't matter. It's the house I'm concerned about, don't you see?"

"I'm afraid I don't."

He could see her reflection in the window. She had abandoned her seductive pose and was sitting as demurely as her nakedness would allow on the edge of the bed. He believed that he could trust himself to sit beside her.

"I told you," she said, "I have a kind of inheritance buried in the cellar. I know where it is, but I need your help to get at it. After that we can stay here or leave, it doesn't really matter. I can send Frank away, or we can drown him in the pond. It's my house, after all. Have you changed your mind? Will you help me?"

He was appalled. He didn't know how to tell her that she was blocking out the truth, or if he should even try. He didn't know whether her lapse of memory was a normal reaction to a traumatic experience, or if it was a symptom of a profound disorder. He had blundered terribly in coming here. Kissing her had only compounded his blunder.

She sighed. "All right." She stared earnestly into his eyes. "I suppose I'll have to tell you the truth."

He had no idea what truth she meant, but he nodded and said, "Please."

"It's difficult. Frank doesn't understand, of course, and neither does Dr. Keller, whom I foolishly told. I hope you will, Rupert. If you really love me as much as you say you do, you will."

He took her hand, carefully avoiding the unexplained bandage, and squeezed her fingers. "I'll try."

"My father was God. No, don't nod your head so readily. I'm not speaking in a figurative sense about his authority or my admiration for him or anything like that. I mean, he was really *God.* He didn't actually create the universe, of course, Azathoth did that by accident, but the Great Old Ones have always needed an emissary in the material world to whom they could grant godlike powers to assist them in their grand design."

Rupert tried hard not to let the horror and despair that he felt show on his face, even though she no longer seemed to see him. She stared fixedly at a point in midair beyond him as she gripped his hand painfully.

"I always felt terribly guilty about it, you have no idea, when my father used to fuck me, but of course then I thought that he was just an ordinary, run of the mill pervert. I didn't understand that common rules of conduct simply didn't apply to him — or to me, either. He didn't realize himself who he was until rather late in life, until it was too late for him to exert his powers fully. He didn't have the books, or the proper keys, or the assistance of the only woman who could have helped him."

"Rose —"

"Please don't interrupt, Rupert, it's difficult enough to explain all this, because I'm dealing with entirely new and startling concepts of the nature of consciousness and the purpose of life on earth. For several centuries, God walked the earth as Mordred Glendower, incarnating himself in a new body each generation. He could pass on not just his powers but his very *self*, his Godhead, to his son, provided that he sired the son on his daughter and followed certain necessary rituals that we needn't go into at the moment. In 1847, the time had come for him to move on to the body of his son once again, but some small-minded busybodies managed to stop him with fire. They also hanged his daughter, Mirdath. The son, who wasn't even aware of his own importance, managed to avoid the mob and wandered off to California, where he tried to behave like a normal human being. He and his descendants married strangers, so the spark of receptivity weakened and was in danger of dying out altogether."

Rose had become totally absorbed in her nonsensical recitation. Sick at heart, Rupert managed to disengage his hand from hers. Slowly, taking infinite pains not to distract her, he got to his feet and began retreating to the door.

"The spark was *very* strong in my father, though. I suppose that a message had been sent to him from Beyond, because he knew that he had to get me with child, that it would be the last chance for the return of Mordred, for the complete reincarnation of God on earth. He may have succeeded with Patrick, I'm not sure, or I may need to have another child with Patrick to concentrate the spark even more. But whatever is necessary, nothing can happen until we retrieve the keys from the cellar, don't you see? There are books there that can tell us everything we need to know, and — what do you think you're doing, Rupert? You're not leaving! I haven't dismissed you!"

"Rose, I think we should . . . think this over. Sleep on it, maybe. You've told me a lot of things that are difficult to digest — entirely new concepts, as you said —"

"Sleep on it?" She sprang to her feet and strutted toward him, hands on hips, head flung back in wild laughter. "You miserable lump of clay, don't you understand that the daughter of God is offering you her love in return for a ridiculously simple task, the work of a moment? What is there to think about? And who are you, worm, to think about such matters?"

"Please, Rose, not so loud —"

"Loud? Do you think that was loud? This is *loud!*" she roared in a voice that had alarmingly descended several octaves. "I'll call down the thunder on your head, you gibbering ape! I'll raise up Crom Cruach from his sleep beneath Stonehenge if you want to hear something *loud!*"

Her voice rose up from the depths of her body with a volume painful to his ears. A great wind had sprung up almost at the same time her roaring tirade had begun. It kept rising in intensity, driving black sheets of rain against the rattling window. At the name "Crom Cruach," uttered in a voice like the bass note of a cathedral organ, a luckily timed peal of thunder shook the house with an ear-splitting cannonade. It seemed just barely possible that Frank hadn't heard her raving above the pandemonium outside.

Abruptly she changed her tactics. She flung herself at his feet, tightly embracing his knees, and gazed up at him with a beseeching look that at the same time exuded raw lechery.

"Please do it, Rupert, please, please, please! I'm begging you. All you have to do is knock a hole in the wall of the cellar. I'll do anything for you — *anything!*"

He wrenched free from her clutches and hurled himself at the door. He struggled with the knob for what seemed an eternity before it gave and he plunged into the dark hallway, where he collided with Frank.

"You fool! You blind, mindless, puritanical fool!" she shrieked after him. "How dare you spurn the favors of the daughter of God?"

"Now, Rupert, don't you feel like a complete asshole? Why don't you mind your own goddamn business?" Frank said wearily, thrusting him aside and continuing down the hall. He called out, "It's all right, pinhead, God's only begotten son-in-law is here. It's time to take your happy pills like a good goddess."

Chapter Ten

*B*efore the door slammed behind Frank, leaving Rupert in total darkness, he heard him singing merrily:

"All of the other writers laughed and shouted out with glee —"

He leaned against the wall, knees shaking, breathing hard. He wanted to stand there forever or, better still, to die there on the spot, but he had to force himself to move before he would have to endure more of Frank's scorn. He fumbled his way down the stairs to the Great Hall.

He berated himself for the fragility of his love. Rose had produced in him the same sort of revulsion he might have felt if, out of an elegant floral arrangement on a snowy tablecloth, a venomous serpent had slithered. His fault was more serious than a failure of love. It was a lack of simple charity. She was ill. If her illness had been physical, no matter what changes it had wrought in her, he was sure he wouldn't have been revolted. In the desert, torn and mangled men rendered incontinent by shock had died beside him, and disgust had never figured in the mix of emotions he'd felt. Yet Rose had disgusted him. He wondered if his love for her could ever be rekindled, even if she were to recover completely.

"Rupert," said a voice at his elbow, and he cried aloud.

"I'm sorry if I startled you," Patrick said.

"Why didn't you tell me?"

"Tell you what?"

"About Rose — her condition."

Patrick gripped his arm. "I thought it best that you find out for yourself. Would you have believed me?" When Rupert made no reply, Patrick said, "You're quite fond of her, aren't you?"

"Yes."

"Don't worry. She'll get the best of care."

Patrick's calm reassured him. Only later did it strike him as odd that such cold, impersonal reassurances should have been given by Rose's son.

"I had hoped to see you before you left." Patrick guided him through the darkness with a hand on his elbow. "Could I impose upon you for a ride?"

"Yes, sure." Rupert moved quickly toward the front door, now that he could see it. Shana, holding an awkward bundle, was silhouetted against it.

"Your coat, Master Rupert!" Patrick called after him as he plunged into the rain.

He turned and accepted it. The night air seemed to clear his head. It was raining lightly, but not at all as it had been when he was in Rose's room. That howling wind had died. He saw that the bundle Shana held appeared to be a shovel wrapped in burlap.

Shana climbed into the back with the shovel as Rupert got behind the wheel. Glancing back at her, he saw that her blouse was torn and there was a dark swelling on her jaw. That was none of his business. He had no right to advise them how to conduct themselves. He vented some of his bitterness and shame on the Laughlins' lawn as he spun the wheels and slewed back onto the driveway.

"Where do you two want to go?"

"We would be obliged if you would take us to the crossing of the High Road with Brookside Lane."

He drove in silence for a while, trying to concentrate on the wet blacktop beyond the swish of his wipers, trying not to think of his encounter with Rose. He felt numb now. He knew that it would hurt later. He thought about Patrick's words, wondering why he had said "High Road" instead of calling it the highway or simply identifying it by its number, as most people would. Then he laughed.

"That's the Mt. Tabor landfill," he said. "The town dump."

"Indeed," Patrick said.

"It's a hell of a place to take your girl on a rainy night in October. With a shovel?"

"A whim," Patrick said. He leaned back to say to Shana, "Love is ever subject to the reign of sportive fancy, is it not, dearest?"

Rupert found Patrick's affectations even more insufferable than his cruelty. He had developed an offbeat variant of an English accent to go with his odd choice of words.

"Look, Patrick, if you want to frolic in the town dump, that's up to you. But why don't you let me take Shana home? She's wet already, and it's getting colder by the minute. She'll wind up with pneumonia."

"I have need of her. Someone must dig."

"Oh, Jesus," Rupert groaned. He tried to catch the girl's eye in the rearview mirror, but her fond gaze was fixed on the back of Patrick's head. "Shana, wouldn't you rather I took you home? Or dropped you both off at a movie or something? This is crazy."

"Why don't you just mind your own fucking business?" Shana said. "I want to do whatever Patrick wants."

"The office of the Good Samaritan has ever been a thankless one," Patrick said.

"It's your funeral."

Patrick laughed loudly. "Quite the opposite."

Rupert resolutely kept his opinions to himself as they drove the last ten minutes. The rain had abated somewhat when he pulled over to the side of the road.

"Here we are. Mt. Tabor landfill. Have fun, kids."

Patrick made no move to get out. He leaned forward to scan the intersection through the windshield.

"This is not the crossroads. There should be an oak tree. . . ."

Rupert impatiently drummed his fingers on the wheel. At last he said, "If you've changed your mind, the offer to take you someplace more sensible is still open."

"No." In a tone suggesting that Rupert was to blame for it, he said: "Back there, the High Road should have curved to the left."

"It used to. Before they straightened it, the highway went through what's now the middle of the town dump."

"The meddlesome swine. Our thanks to you, Master Rupert. We will bid you goodnight then."

Rupert watched them trudge across the road. Their appearance belied Patrick's flippant explanation: the last thing they looked like was a pair of young lovers on a lark. Patrick, limping slightly — and maybe that explained why he couldn't do the digging himself, although what he would be digging for in the first place defied speculation — ignored the girl who trailed behind him in total submission with the shovel over her shoulder. Rupert rejected the idea of following them and making one last appeal to reason. They had both made it clear that his suggestions were unwelcome. He drove home.

He had hoped to get to his room unnoticed and spend some time sorting out his disordered thoughts and feelings, but his father called out to him as he passed the open door of his study.

"Are you all right, Dad?" he asked, but the question was unnecessary. Slumped in his chair at his rolltop desk, George Spencer looked ghastly.

"It's been a very trying day, Rupert. Please have a seat. Very trying. And I just had a most distressing phone conversation with Frank Laughlin."

"He called you?"

"No, I called him on a matter of the utmost urgency, but he immediately launched into an emotional harangue about your antics. I was unable to impress on him the importance of what I had to say." He smiled wryly. "He told me, in his characteristically colorful way, to go piss up a rope."

"I guess I rubbed him the wrong way," Rupert said. He felt that he didn't owe his father an explanation of his conduct, but he volunteered one: "I had to see for myself that Rose was genuinely ill. She is. My visit upset her."

"So Frank told me. You couldn't have picked a worse time, but you've always had a gift for romantic misadventures."

"I think —" Rupert began heatedly.

"Oh, do sit down and be quiet. I'm not going to lecture you about your obsession for ferreting out unsuitable women. I wanted to talk to you about burglarizing Frank's house."

"Good God." He knew that George's words had been calculated to shock him and arouse his curiosity, and they did. He sat down.

"I'm quite serious. Frank is sitting on a bomb, but he refuses to believe it — refuses even to listen to me. I always thought the man was a fool. So we have to find a way of removing the bomb for his own protection."

"What do you mean by a bomb?"

"You're the only person I can take into my confidence, although you're probably the least likely person on earth to believe me. You may think I'm crazy. I can only beg you to indulge me, as your father, in my eccentricity."

"I've done a lot of that for other people this evening. Sure, why not you, too?"

George swiveled his chair to face him directly. His expression was intensely serious, even grave.

"I've been on the phone for the past six hours, listening to lies, evasions, half-truths, hints, and threats, and I've come to the conclusion that there exists an unlikely conspiracy of scholars, literary men, and theoretical physicists to conceal certain information from the vast majority of the human race."

George's hard stare was an invitation to comment or question. Rupert said, "Unlikely, yes. What have scholars and literary men got in common with theoretical physicists?"

George flashed what Rupert and Madge called his villainous smile. "Academic credentials and connections. They're all members of the same club, they all wear the old school tie. It remained for a self-educated, quirky genius, a man who didn't even go to high school, to let the cat out of the bag. Fortunately for the conspiracy — perhaps fortunately for all of us — he did it in such an idiosyncratic way that the world at large didn't take him seriously. He used the information he had — and he didn't have all of it — as a peg on which to hang the plots of a series of horror stories."

"Oh, come on, Dad," Rupert said, and his eyes drifted toward the bookcase that housed the material of his father's screwball hobby. "Are you talking about H.P. Lovecraft?"

George nodded. "Oddly enough, he knew exactly what he was doing in leaking the information. He was rather playfully tweaking the academic community that wanted no part of him and, in a darker way, flirting with the destruction of the twentieth-century world that he detested so profoundly. I had it this afternoon from a thoroughly reliable source that when *The Call of Cthulhu* was first printed in 1928, Albert Einstein panicked. He had drafted a letter urging Farnsworth Wright, Lovecraft's editor, in the strongest possible terms, not to print any more stories on similar themes, but cooler heads prevailed and convinced him that the best way of dealing with Lovecraft was to ignore him completely."

"Good advice. He was the world's worst writer, in addition to being a nut."

"This isn't a literary debate. I'm aware of your wrong-headed opinion of his style. It's the truth of his content that concerns us here." Nettled by Rupert's remark, George had spoken with some heat. He now tried to make amends by offering him one of his Havana cigars, a rare gesture. He lit one himself before continuing: "As I said, Lovecraft knew just what he was doing. He knew that his information was — well, dangerous is an inadequate word when we're dealing with the possibility of a catastrophic change in the nature of the universe, an alteration of its physical laws — but anyway, he knew that his information was dangerous. As a genius, he had naturally attracted a circle of devoted disciples, young writers who imitated his style and borrowed his themes. He corresponded volumi-nously with them, but never once did he so much as hint to any of them that the knowledge he possessed was anything but a figment of his own imagination. Soon a dozen or more little hacklets were churning out stories that alluded to the Great Old Ones and the *Necronomicon,* blissfully unaware of the apoplectic seizures and heart attacks they were provoking in the ivied halls from Oxford to Harvard."

Rupert convulsively snapped his cigar in two. Only gradually did the shock on his father's face draw his attention to what he had done.

"Dad." He had to pause to bring his voice under full control. "Rose was raving about the Great Old Ones this afternoon. I didn't recognize the source of that phrase at the time. It seems to be the focus of her — her illness."

George shielded his eyes with his hand for a moment. "For my part, I don't need any more proof," he said at last, "but perhaps that will be enough to convince you to keep an open mind about all this and hear me out fully. Rose is in danger, too. We all are. I was guilty of under-statement when I said that Frank is sitting on a bomb, Rupert. He's sitting on the Doomsday Machine."

"Maybe if you tried to get to the point —"

"Let me tell you in my own way. After his death, Lovecraft's disciples still didn't realize that they were playing with a potentially cataclysmic truth. Not even the suicide of his literary executor, a young man named Robert Barlow who'd had posthumous access to his secret files, aroused their suspicions. It became clear to the members of the conspiracy that the writers making glib references to Hastur and Yog-Sothoth and the ineffable Dr. John Dee were doing so in ignorance, like children who merrily chant 'Ring Around the Rosie' without the faintest notion that they are reciting an ancient charm to ward off the Black Death.

"Someone — it may have been the CIA — paid off his posthumous publisher, August Derleth, to trivialize his concepts and make a hash of his unpublished fragments. The conspirators breathed easy until another self-taught genius, a man with no standing in their world, dropped the other shoe. He had read Lovecraft's stories, recognized the truths swimming dimly in their depths, and aggressively sought out the facts. Then, in the playfully suicidal tradition of Lovecraft, he wove the facts into works of ostensible fiction. He caused a few more heart attacks when he disclosed the existence of the Voynich Manuscript at the University of Pennsylvania. I determined today that there really is such a manuscript, a medieval key or guide to the *Necronomicon.*"

"And this other — ah — initiate is?"

"Colin Wilson. It's amusing to note that some of Lovecraft's fanatical devotees have berated Wilson roundly for perverting the Gospel according to Lovecraft — not realizing, of course, that Wilson had gone back to the original sources for his information. I was told that some of our foremost academics advocated Wilson's assassination at some point, but they were overruled."

"What has all this got to do with Frank Laughlin?"

"The point of all this, Rupert, is that Frank has a copy of the *Necronomicon* in his cellar."

Rupert studied his broken cigar gloomily. His father made the unprecedented offer of a second one. He smoked in silence, aware that his father was watching him and awaiting his considered reaction.

He was reluctant to entertain the idea that his father had gone mad, too, but it was an inescapable possibility. Madness — extreme forms of hysteria, at least — could be contagious, and he had already considered that as an explanation for the conduct of the Laughlins and Shana Jennings. George had reinforced the idea inadvertently by his reference to the Black Death. Some survivors of the plague had developed an irresistible compulsion to dance in the streets, sometimes dancing until they dropped dead of exhaustion.

One medieval example of mass insanity suggested another one, the affliction known as St. Anthony's Fire. It was caused by consuming ergot, a fungus of rye with hallucinogenic properties similar to those of LSD. It was uncommon in modern times, but someone with a preference for organically-grown, chemically-untreated grains, someone who stored the flour in a rather dank place and baked her own bread — someone like Rose, in fact — could unsuspectingly whip up a batch of rye bread with a medieval curse on it. Home-baked rye had been on the buffet table at the Hallowe'en party.

The similarity between Rose's delusions and George's — yes, George's delusions, he had to face up to the words — could be explained simply. H.P. Lovecraft, an inept writer of silly trash, had been George's lifelong hobby. He collected the man's books, researched his life, made occasional excursions to Providence, Rhode Island, and other cities to visit his old haunts. To the embarrassment of his loved ones, he even attended fan conventions, where he appeared on panels as an expert.

Rupert and his mother had always considered his avocation a harmless, even a lovable, quirk. If he had gone crazy, it was only logical that he should have done so along the path of an existing preoccupation. The madmen who fancied themselves to be Napoleon had no doubt been Napoleonic scholars in their saner days. George could have given Rose an earful of Cthulhu and Yog-Sothoth and the *Necronomicon* at the party, and she'd used it as a convenient framework for her own psychosis. LSD heightened one's susceptibility to suggestion, and perhaps ergot did, too. He would have to do some research in the town library tomorrow.

Everyone's craziness could be traced back to the party. He made a mental note to call some other guests tomorrow and question them tactfully. Thinking of the other guests reminded him of Ashcroft and his gang. Ergot, fly agaric, and other hallucinogens found in nature had always been the stock in trade of witches, and that's what Ashcroft and his followers professed to be. Some drug could have been deliberately introduced into the food or drink.

"You seem to be giving the subject an awful lot of thought, Rupert. Would you give me the benefit of it?"

"Oh. Yes. Excuse me." He made a production out of flicking the long ash from his cigar and savoring a mouthful of smoke while he tried to think of a comment that might satisfy his father. "Well, as you said yourself, Frank is a fool. Even if he does have the book, it's unlikely that he'll make use of it. He probably doesn't appreciate its significance."

George nodded. "I explained its significance to him, but I could see that he didn't take me seriously. It's not him that I'm worried about. It's Patrick. He believes that he is the reincarnation of the evil man who assembled that library, and I have no doubt he'll try to work some mischief with it."

Now that he had developed a theory to explain why their delusions dovetailed so neatly, Rupert wasn't surprised to hear George echoing Rose's fantasies of reincarnation. He wondered if his father could tell him what Patrick might be doing in the town dump, but he hesitated to mention that for fear of alarming him. He decided to risk telling part of the truth.

"I was talking to Patrick this evening, and he questioned me about the route of the old highway. Do you know if the old intersection of the highway with Brookside Lane has any special significance? Where the town dump is now?"

He suppressed a smile when he saw that his father, despite his worry about the imminent destruction of the universe, could still be diverted by a question addressed to his other pastime, local history.

"Oh, yes. Public hangings were held there as late as 1815 or thereabouts, and the area was used as a potter's field for another twenty years or so. None of this came to light until after the highway was rerouted and the dump was in use, so it caused quite a stir at the time. Since none of the graves had been marked or recorded, not much could be done to relocate them, and the furor eventually abated. Did he suggest that someone named Mirdath Hodgson might have been buried there?"

"Not directly. But wasn't she hanged in 1847?"

"She was? How do you know?"

"Why . . . Rose told me."

"It's not unlikely. Even though the oak tree at that crossroads was no longer an official site for executions, her hanging had no legal sanction, as far as I know. A crossroads was traditionally held to be an ideal place to bury a witch or a vampire, and she was believed to be both. But this is all beside the point. We have to work out a plan for getting that book out of the mill tonight."

Rupert nodded thoughtfully, suspecting that direct resistance to that piece of lunacy would be useless. He would have to think of a more subtle way to dissuade his father.

"Have you told any of the members of the . . . ah . . . conspiracy where the book is? Maybe if they knew, they'd grab the ball and run with it." He wanted to add that Stephen Hawking might be the ideal man for the job, but he forced himself to maintain the proper air of seriousness.

"There isn't time. We're already here on the scene, and we can get the book tonight. I suggest that we both go, ostensibly to apologize to Frank for your earlier visit. While you engage him in conversation, I'll ask to use the bathroom off the kitchen, then slip downstairs and get the book. I know exactly where it is."

"And then you'll sneak it out under your coat, eh? I assume this is the pocket edition of the *Necronomicon.*"

"You're quite right, of course, the damned thing is as big as the Manhattan phone book. Well, I could toss it out one of the kitchen windows, and we could retrieve it later."

"There's one other thing wrong with your plan. Frank will know exactly who swiped it, and how. The best idea would be for me to sneak into the house alone and take it."

George was alarmed. "That would be a felony! If we're invited into the house, I could argue —"

"I'm sure that's not how a successful crook thinks, Dad. Our only concern should be getting away undetected with the goods. The only way

I can be caught is in the act of stealing the book, with Frank as the only witness against me, and I could throw up an effective smoke screen by saying I'd broken into his house to see his wife. But he's probably passed out by now, so he won't catch me. Another thing you might consider is that you have far too much to lose by getting involved in this. I'm safe; I never heard of a writer being disbarred."

George chuckled, and Rupert congratulated himself on his tactics. He believed he had struck just the right note of serious intent and judicious deliberation to convince his father that he could be entrusted with the job. The only problem that remained was what to do now. He couldn't return empty-handed. Nor was George crazy enough to believe that a copy of the phone book he'd mentioned was really the *Necronomicon*. Yet there was no such book, in Frank's house or anywhere else.

"Still, Rupert, this is my idea — my obsession, if you must. I can see that I haven't really communicated to you my sense of urgency, my belief in the overwhelming importance of this task."

His self-congratulation had been premature. George still wavered. He decided to try absolute candor. "You asked me at first to indulge you, as my father, in your eccentricity. I said I would, and I am, because your story hasn't really convinced me. But don't you believe that my respect and affection for you are strong enough motives for me to try my best? If that book is there, Dad, I'll get it for you."

"Very well, Rupert, you win," George said with his most villainous smile. "I suggest, though, that you wait a few hours until they're all asleep."

Rupert shook his head as he got up and stretched. "Now is the perfect time. Rose is under sedation. So is Frank, probably, in his own way. Patrick is . . . ah . . . out on a date. It's still raining hard enough to muffle any noise I might make. It's a big house with thick, stone walls, and none of them — well, Patrick, maybe, but he's out — is very concerned about locking the doors and windows."

He was in such a rush to take his leave that he forgot his trenchcoat, and the rain was now splattering down with the mushy consistency of incipient sleet. His wool turtleneck — white, unfortunately, no burglar's costume — wasn't heavy enough for comfort, but his only desire after getting out of the house was to stay out. He hurried into his car and started the engine, cursing the sluggishness of the heater.

He considered his options as he drove to the highway. If he went to Dr. Keller now with his half-baked theory of drugs administered by witches, the most he could expect would be a pat on the shoulder, a prescription for Valium, and an enormous bill. He could take that step only after he had questioned a significant sampling of the other guests at the party and researched the properties of ergot and other likely drugs.

He was struck by a new and chilling thought. He had eaten breakfast on Saturday, then spent the rest of the day doing research for a magazine piece at the library. He had run home with only time to change into his costume and had arrived at the party with a wolfish appetite. He'd sampled everything at the buffet table. If his theory was correct, he might notice at any minute that his fingers had turned into fluorescent green snakes.

Nobody had yet confessed to seeing green snakes, however. The victims had thus far exhibited only symptoms of paranoia: delusions of grandeur, fears of insidious conspiracies. He examined his own mind for such symptoms and found none, but of course that proved nothing. He firmly believed that he was a tall, blond young man with regular features and an athletic build, and that he was at this moment driving his lovingly-restored red Camaro Z/28 along a rainswept highway in Connecticut. But how could he prove that this wasn't an illusion, that he wasn't really a toad in the bottom of a well, dreaming of this apparent reality? He found this fancy unsettling.

Without conscious choice, he had pointed his car toward the Laughlins' mill. He knew then that he would carry out the crazy burglary. Having promised his father, he had no choice. He had a roll of duct-tape in the trunk. If he found the doors locked, he would tape up a pane of a kitchen window, break it, and peel the glass off soundlessly with the tape, as he had seen done in the movies. It would take three minutes to run down to the cellar and determine that there was no *Necronomicon* in the secret room, if there was indeed a secret room. On the other hand, he might find it sitting fat and evil in the middle of the room: in which case he would have proof that he shared in the general madness. He didn't care for that fancy, either.

He was about to pass the town dump. He pulled to the side of the road on sudden impulse and cut off his lights and engine. He had dropped off Patrick and Shana nearly an hour ago. How long would it take them to exhume a body? He feared that they still might be out there, wandering crazed and half-frozen in a treacherous wasteland. He now profoundly regretted his irresponsibility in leaving them here. True, he had been rattled by his interview with Rose, and both Patrick and Shana had provoked him with their incivility, but those seemed flimsy excuses for his lapse. The inescapable fact remained that he'd abandoned them.

He snapped open the glove compartment to get his flashlight. His hand lingered for a moment on the butt of the pistol he also kept there. He seized the flashlight and snapped the compartment shut, wondering if the urge to take the gun with him had been his first identifiable symptom of paranoia. It wouldn't be a bad idea, once he got home, to unload the gun for good and bury it in the bottom of his foot-locker with his camouflage fatigues. Some day he would dig it out to show as a curiosity to his grandchildren, but they would be too preoccupied with the news of the latest interplanetary laser-war on three-dimensional television to pay him any attention.

He shoved the flashlight into his back pocket as he crossed the road. It was unnecessary at the moment. The wet night was luminous with diffused light from distant towns and turnpikes. Even in this isolated spot a dull, subliminal hum of tires and machines filled the air. He tried to stay on the former path of Brookside Lane, but it was difficult to discern in a landscape of shapeless humps and hollows. His boots crunched glass and metal and sank in muck. He was uncomfortably cold, but in one way he was thankful for that: the cold subdued the odor of the place.

"Patrick!" he called. "Shana!"

He thought of calling Mirdath and Mordred, but he was amused to note that he didn't have the requisite courage. Maybe this was another sign that the universal paranoia was infecting him.

He heard a noise far to his left, a slithering accompanied by a rattle of tumbling cans. He stopped and reached for his flashlight, then thought better of it. He would spoil his night vision.

"Hey, Patrick!" he trumpeted through his hands. "Sha-naaa!"

The silence oppressed him. He walked on, bearing to the left now. Under the rubbish he crunched lay the graves of hanged men and paupers. He wondered about them. They used to hang people for sneezing in church, just about. Had they really hanged Mirdath for being a witch? He had always thought of New England in 1847 as a hotbed of liberalism, with Thoreau refusing to pay his taxes to finance a war he'd considered immoral. But if you looked hard enough, you could probably find pockets of ignorance and superstition anywhere, in any age.

The thought inspired him to yell, "Mirdath!" and "Mordred!"

He heard a rustling that wasn't the sleet and directed his steps more sharply to the left. He hesitated. Not only had he lost the course of Brookside Lane, he was uncertain of the location of the highway and his car. It hadn't even occurred to him that one could get lost in so insignificant a plot as the Mt. Tabor landfill, but he was in fact lost. Humps of unfamiliar sameness rose on every hand. He didn't panic. Cars would eventually pass on the highway, and he would see at least the glow of their lights. If that failed, there was a brook in here somewhere. Following it would bring him out. But it was cold, and his worry for Patrick and Shana increased.

"Yog-Sothoth!" he shouted, and the sleet seemed to fall a little harder.

He decided to climb one of the taller hummocks and reconnoiter the area. It proved a bad idea. He hadn't sensed how fragile was the structure of the apparently solid shadow. Debris shifted beneath him. He fell sprawling twice. He could stand being wet, but not being smeared with wet, unidentifiable muck. At last he stood on top of the unstable pile, and he believed he could make out a line of trees that marked the far side of the highway.

"Sha — NA!" he roared. "Patrick!"

They had hitchhiked home long ago, of course, they were tucked in with their teddy bears and their visions of sugar plums, while a lone idiot howled in a garbage dump and the sleet cascaded down on his head. But what if Patrick's body were found here, stiff and blue, in the morning? He had failed Rose once. He had failed her again by marooning her son in this lunar wilderness.

He looked down and saw something at the bottom of the hummock that seemed too white and pure to belong here. He strained his eyes against the darkness, then pulled out his light and flicked it briefly over the object. It could have been the sleeve of Shana's white school-sweater. He picked his way cautiously down the queasy face of the heap. He knew, intellectually, that finding a torn piece of clothing was not a good sign, but his principal emotion was relief at finding something, anything at all.

He stooped to pick it up. It was unaccountably heavy, and he thought for a moment that his identification had been wrong. Then he saw why it was so heavy. The sleeve contained an arm, with the white and splintered bone protruding from one end.

"The police," he muttered aloud. "I'm going to get the police."

He was unable to act. He didn't want to leave the grisly relic. He had the feeling that nobody would ever be able to find it again in this mess. Nor could he take it with him. That would be tampering with evidence, disturbing the scene of a crime. At last he used his flashlight to scan the area. He found a curiously misshapen human ribcage festooned with pale shreds. It nestled on a patch of white wool that looked like another fragment of her sweater.

He crept closer. He would have been willing to bet that Shana's ribcage, in life, had not been *misshapen*. He bent down and touched it. These appeared to be human ribs, but they had lost their solidity. They were rubbery.

He walked away down the gully, fanning the light before him. If Patrick had done that, he'd used an explosive device. He could think of no alternative. A high-speed auto wreck could do that to a human body, or a plane crash, but she couldn't have been involved in either. Unquestionably, it had been an explosion. Patrick probably had nothing to do with it. Somebody must have cleaned out his attic and unthinkingly discarded a souvenir hand grenade with the trash.

Despite that reasonable explanation, he was still troubled by the condition of the human fragments. The arm had been unnaturally soft, even mushy, and the flesh and bone had appeared translucent. The bones of the ribcage had appeared translucent, too, and to have lost their rigidity. The rubbery feel of those bones still crawled on his fingertips. He was tempted to go back and make a closer inspection, but not tempted strongly enough.

He was jerked into alertness. He thought his light had fallen on a woman's face. He flashed it back, saw no one. He regretted that he had become dependent on the light. He moved forward. He became aware of a nauseating stench. That, of course, was only to be expected in a garbage dump, but he had noticed no intolerable odors before.

He could proceed no further. The loathsome fetor blocked his passage like a material wall. It suggested a sweltering beach piled high with long-dead creatures of the sea. Still the sleet hissed down. He stumbled back the way he had come, but the air got no better. He looked to either side for a way of escape from the odor, but he stood in a trench with precipitous walls. His mouth filled with bile. He gagged and spat, fighting down the rebellion of his stomach. His flashlight was no longer of much use, for his vision was clouded by his tears.

A soft hand took him gently by the arm. "Patrick," he wanted to say, but he could make only retching noises as the noxious reek grew impossibly strong. Another hand caressed his cheek. He shook the tears from his eyes and looked into a female face of almost alarming loveliness. Around him he heard a rustling, as of a squamous hide slithering over rocks, but he could ignore it as he gazed into her dark and deep-set eyes. He reached out to stroke her hair. In the glow of the flashlight, fallen and forgotten in the muck, he could see that it was a curious shade of dark red.

She spoke — no, she made a sound, at once a hiss and a throaty growl. It broke the spell. He questioned who and even what she was. He tried to twist out of her embrace, but her soft fingers, impossibly, seemed to be wrapped more than once around his arm, and they became vises of steel. Unbearable pressure forced him to his knees in the slime.

Where there should have been the smoothness of a woman's legs, there was the coarseness of animal hair. Where human knees would have bent outward, these bent inward like the knees of a beast. He screamed as he saw, amid the steely bristles, dozens, no, hundreds of tiny red orifices, pulsating and sucking, opening and closing, throbbing and quivering with pustulant life, each of them surrounded with questing, furry tendrils. He was yanked inward, screaming, to those mouths, to the oozing sources of the abominable odor.

He could no longer scream, for one of the mouths had clamped over his, and he felt his teeth dissolving in the overflow of its acid slime. He fought maniacally, thrusting out with his fists, but their impact on scales and bristles was unaccountably soft and ineffective. Then he saw that the solid flesh of his hands and arms, with each blow he struck, were being transformed into a milky, mucilaginous jelly.

He wondered if he were at last experiencing the hallucinations for which he had steeled himself; but he knew that no hallucination could ever have hurt so much.

Chapter Eleven

*P*atrick woke up with the sense that something was horribly wrong. Afternoon sunlight filtered through the window of his bedroom. He looked down and saw that he was still wearing his damp, filthy clothes. He remembered what was wrong.

Even though he couldn't sense Mordred's presence in his mind, he took the precaution of thinking about a catchy, popular song and letting its inane melody run continuously in his head before turning his attention to serious matters. He had learned that Mordred couldn't see through even so flimsy a defense. Without that defense, he would have been punished with a pain like a dentist's drill in his skull for daring to think forbidden thoughts: which included any thoughts about Mordred and his doings.

He needed his glasses. That was a good sign. Maybe Mordred was asleep. Maybe he had gone for good or lost his hold, but that was too much to hope for. It hurt when he got up and walked, but the pain was his own, the result of his exertions in the dump last night. It wasn't the pain of Mordred's ineptly set leg, broken during his headlong flight from Salem, Massachusetts, in 1692.

The book lay open on his desk, the pages freshly smeared by his own muddy hands as Mordred had searched desperately to find out what had gone wrong and how it might be made right. He shook his head at this fresh vandalism of the irreplaceable book. Mordred's gross carelessness in so many things was a trait hard to reconcile with his age and presumed wisdom. He had run out of the house with the page torn from the *Necronomicon* bearing the appropriate incantation, but he hadn't even bothered to read beyond it, to the passage warning that the bones to be raised should be free from "forraine contamination."

In his four hundred years of life, whatever good qualities he might have possessed had atrophied, leaving nothing but a vacuum of selfishness that demanded instant gratification. Patrick wondered if ultimate maturity meant a return to the mindless wanting of a newborn infant, or if Mordred were a special case on account of his basic wickedness. He shuddered to remember in sickening detail the fantasies his jaded appetites had forced poor Shana to bring to life.

He had forgotten to think of the song. *I love you, you love me. . . .* He played it again in his mind, exaggerating the simple beat, while he sat down and began to turn the pages of the book, looking for a spell that would get rid of Mordred forever.

Without willing it, he found himself closing the book and rising to his feet. He took off his glasses. Mordred had returned. Patrick remembered to keep the tune playing on the surface of his consciousness. Mordred accepted without question that Patrick was a brainless juvenile. He was grossly underestimating him, Patrick believed, and he might be able to use that as a weapon to destroy him.

He limped up to Frank's studio and stood at the door unnoticed, watching him paint. It was a lovely portrait of Mirdath, but the sight of it enraged Mordred for not being able to see her in the flesh like that. His attitude toward her was curious. He lusted for her — but he lusted for anything young and warm, whether it was male, female or animal. He was afraid of her, too. He respected her. Apparently in life she had possessed knowledge and basic talents that were utterly beyond him, but which he needed to encompass fully his dark designs.

"Was she not beautiful?" he said coldly, startling Frank.

"Oh, hi, Patrick. Can you see her at all without your glasses?"

"I can see everything. I can see the past, present, and future, the secrets of Inner Earth and the mysteries of the lich and coffin-worm. I know where the Great Old Ones lie or lurk, and I know how to rouse them."

Frank regarded him sourly. "Very funny, I'm sure, but I'd go a little easy on that bullshit with strangers. George Spencer, for one, thinks you're nuts." He paused to study his work for a moment. "He called me again this morning to ask about Rupert, who has apparently disappeared. They found his car abandoned by the town dump."

"Perhaps," Mordred sniggered, "he has become absorbed in some new lover."

Frank gave him a bleak look, but he said: "That seems like the most plausible explanation, considering that it's Rupert. George was quite upset, though, and he seems to think that his disappearance has something to do with that screwy book. Maybe I should give him the damned thing just to get him off our backs."

"Maybe I will arrange a meeting for you with your subject."

"Huh?"

"I said, I may introduce you to the subject of your portrait. You would be ravished by her," Mordred said, turning and limping out.

Frank followed him to the stairs and called out, "Do me a favor, huh? Don't go bothering Rose with that crap. She's bad enough as it is."

Not looking back, Mordred waved Patrick's hand in a gesture of indifference. Still floating the silly melody in front of his thoughts, Patrick wondered if Mordred meant what he said. He was angry enough, certainly, but his rage wasn't directed specifically at Frank.

Mordred turned his attention to Patrick: *Where may I find a stout cudgel?*

Patrick considered, then slipped an answer through his musical screen: *There's a baseball bat downstairs in the closet near the front door.*

He wondered if he could probe Mordred's mind. He was afraid to try. In the first few hours of his complete takeover, Mordred had trained him mercilessly. He could no more have extended a mental probe toward the wizard's thoughts than he could have reached out to touch a fire with his bare hand. But he would have to try. He couldn't spend the rest of his life cringing in a narrow corner of his own consciousness, shivering with fear and loathing while he observed Mordred abusing his body and torturing others. He would fight . . . but not just yet.

Mordred, still radiating a dull glow of rage, went to the closet and rummaged through it until he found the bat. He hefted it, slapped it down against his palm, seemed satisfied. Reading the incised inscription, he wanted to know who "Ty Cobb" was, but Patrick himself didn't know. He went down to the cellar. He needed no light as he made his sure-footed way to the door of the secret room, now closed. The snake-pit odor seeped through even the tight joints of the stones and hung before the door in a tangible miasma.

Mordred pressed the right combination of stones. The door grated inward. He descended from darkness to blackness and stench.

"Father," rasped an inhuman voice, and something caressed his cheek.

Mordred swung the bat down in a short, vicious arc. It thumped soundly against something soft and solid. The blow provoked a shriek with chittering, ratlike overtones.

"Stupid slut," Mordred growled, fumbling for matches in Patrick's pockets. "Keep your putrid paws off me."

Mordred lit the candles and turned to face the freakish mass that hulked, trembling, in a corner. Patrick wanted to keep his eyes fixed on the face, even more beautiful than it had been in his dreams. Mordred wanted to survey the entirety of the abomination. As soon as he felt Patrick's reflexive resistance, he gave him the mental equivalent of a chop with the bat. Patrick screamed in his mind.

"Father, please," it whimpered, "send me back to my grave."

"Your grave, and the grave of cats and rats and goats and serpents and whatever other carcass was thrown there or crawled there to die! Lascivious bitch! Sharing your final bed with every beast of the field!" he roared, and he lunged forward to attack the shivering monstrosity with the bat, striking it forehand and back again and again as he screamed curses at it.

"Let me die again," it groaned. "Let me draw the earth over my bones once more."

Gasping for breath, hands burning from the force of his blows, Mordred slumped in the chair.

"You will tell me the things you know and I do not," he said when he had caught Patrick's breath. "That sniveling craven Dee had not the courage to set forth all in his translation. I must know the last Nine Words of the Ten Words that are the Litany of Hastur. I must know the time and place of the visitations of Shub-Niggurath. I must know how to summon That Which Is (Not)."

"I know these things not, father."

"You know them, you idle harlot! You know them!" Mordred raged.

"I know nothing, father. I know nothing except that I hunger. Give me to eat. Or better still, kill me. Let me go back into the earth where I belong."

Mordred raged incoherently, spattering foam with his curses as he clubbed the thing with all his force. Patrick couldn't understand why it merely cowered and accepted this treatment. He had seen it kill Shana and obliterate Rupert, each in a matter of two or three minutes. It had no logical reason to fear Mordred. He believed that it held back only through a habit of filial devotion. He suspected that Mordred could, in an excess of characteristic carelessness, break that habit. He summoned up his courage and tried to warn Mordred of that, but he was rewarded with a jagged lance of pain.

"If I give you food, whore, will you speak?" Mordred panted. "Will you tell me what I would know?"

"I know nothing, father, save that I hunger and thirst," it sobbed. "Perchance I will know of these matters when I have fed."

"Go then to the top of the house, and tell the clown that you will find there that you are the subject of his portrait. And while you are feasting, look upon yourself as you should be, misbegotten spawn of corruption!"

"Don't go!" Patrick forced his lips to say. "No! Stay — away — from —"

The pain came. It built. It kept building. Patrick faced it and endured it. The dentist's drill in his skull became a jackhammer. Mordred tried to speak, but Patrick refused to let him. Enraged beyond all reason, Mordred tried to strangle him with his own hands. The body that they shared flailed from side to side and caromed off the walls in a desperate struggle with itself. The beast cowered, bewildered.

The pain suddenly stopped. Patrick braced himself for a new onslaught, but it didn't come. Instead Mordred spoke to him in a mental tone so oily and false that Patrick was almost forced to laugh. He threw up the veil of music to keep Mordred from knowing his reaction or reading his real thoughts.

— You are a clever lad, and far stronger than I had thought. A winsome little catch you play in your mind to keep me at a distance! We must someday have a discourse on the pleasures of music. I have heard many a good tune in my long lifetime, and I am no novice at the lute and virginals. Purcell was a friend of mine, and asked my advice on his final tribute to Queen Anne. My skills are yours, Patrick, and music is but the least of them. You can share in my sorceries. You can have women, Patrick, any woman you want. Did you not enjoy our dalliance with Mistress Jennings?

— You killed her.

— Not I, 'twas yonder baggage made a meal of her. You will learn that no woman ever born was worth more than an hour of a man's precious time, and we had a surfeit of that dull creature. But if you wish to punish this excrescence for her gluttony, I will stand aside and let you strike the blows.

— It's going to turn on you. On us. If you have any sense at all, you'll stop tormenting it.

Patrick felt the dull fury of Mordred's frustration pressing in on him. He prepared himself for more torture, but it was withheld.

"I would eat," the thing groaned.

"And so you will, dear child, indeed you will," Mordred said. "But I have held conclave with my young host, and he is unwilling to sacrifice his beloved father to your greedy gut. We will find you another food, fear not, and you can ponder the Litany of Hastur while you wait for it. Hunger may sharpen your wits."

Patrick shivered as Mordred stepped forward to kiss it on the lips and it caressed him with a scaly appendage Then he turned and mounted the stairs while it sighed and babbled of its hunger behind them.

Turning up the volume of his mental music, Patrick pondered his success. He had no idea why Mordred had buckled. It was possible that he had done so merely to lull his vigilance, to soften him for a much more determined attempt at total domination. He refused to consider it a triumph. He would not succumb to the overconfidence that was one of Mordred's faults.

— Who will be her next meal, if not your father?

That was a question Patrick had dreaded.

— Does it have to be a human being? Can't we feed it a steak? Or a cow, for that matter?

— She must feed on human flesh. I propose that the flesh not be ours. She will sooner turn on us from hunger than from any offense I might give to her delicate sensibilities with your — what is it? Your baseball bat. So make your choice. I would suggest we feed her the solicitor who seems to know so much of our doings.

— No. Not after Rupert.

— Choose! She will not be denied much longer, look you. A stone wall is nothing to her hunger, and she might think your darling mother a toothsome morsel.

— God, no! Mrs. Minotaur. . . .

— A wise choice. A splendid choice, enough meat on her bones to keep the willful slut glutted till the morrow. Shall we have the daughter, too, for our own pleasure?

— No!

— Patrick, you are softer than a maiden. I must harden you.

Patrick tried to ignore what Mordred was doing to his body. He played his mental music even louder, drowning out Mordred's evil cackle.

In the kitchen, Patrick stood staring at the phone for a long time. Mordred merely waited, not pushing him. The choice was simple enough: either he would let the thing in the cellar go hungry, in which case it would burst through the wall and devour his parents, or he would try to lure Jane Miniter to her death. He dialed her number.

"Miniter Realty, Jane Miniter speaking."

"Hello, Jane, this is Patrick Laughlin. How are you?"

"Oh, Patrick, what a coincidence! I was just thinking of giving Rose a buzz when you called. I've been telling her that there must be something wrong with a man like Rupert Spencer, who'd still live with his parents at his age — sponge off them, actually. He's never had a proper job since he came back from the army, despite his pretensions of being a writer. He could scarcely support himself on his own by selling a couple of articles a year to the kind of regional New England magazines that you buy in feed stores, could he? But of course Rose won't hear a word against him, she says that he's working on 'something serious,' whatever that might. . ."

Patrick let her rattle on. Without interruption, she might do so for an hour, postponing the moment when he would have to say something that would entice her to her death. Mordred had grown fretful and impatient, and now Patrick could no longer sense his presence inside his skull. He wondered where he went at such times. Perhaps he had no real existence outside their shared body and had always shared it, a dormant aberration in his genetic code. Or perhaps he was a mere illusion, a part of his own personality that he had given a fictitious life of its own. He found it hard to credit that explanation. If Mordred was a figment of his imagination, where had the thing in the cellar come from?

". . . the most outrageous story about Rupert. It seems that he's run off with a high school girl."

Jane's last words caught his attention, and now her silence invited comment.

"Who?"

"That's what I'm trying to tell you. It's the very same girl who came to the party with those hoodlums that Amy was flirting with, Shana Jennings. Nobody saw them run away together, but they're both missing, and that strikes me as all too suggestive a coincidence, don't you agree? I suppose they met at your party. It's not your fault, of course, but there must have been something in the air at that party. Amy's been simply impossible ever since. I expect any day now that she'll run off to join Howard Ashcroft's commune. She must have been confused, or else Frank was drunk, but she seems to think she has an offer from your father to pose in the nude —"

Jane broke off and put her hand over the phone to speak to someone else. She came back: "That was none other than Her Serene Highness, demanding to speak to you, having eavesdropped on our conversation. I told her that no young man in his right mind would want to talk to *her* on the telephone, but she's quite insistent. I wonder if you'd let me speak to Rose first? I'll be quite brief; I just don't have the time today to let her chew my ear off."

"That's one of the reasons I called you. Rose is quite ill. She's under sedation and can't speak to anyone."

"Ill? Sedation?" She annoyed him by instantly intuiting the truth: "Good heavens, Patrick, do you mean that she's lost her mind? When did all this happen?"

"As you said, there must have been something in the air at the party. It was that night."

"Oh. You don't suppose it's because Rupert — no, I shouldn't even have thought that, I'll bite my tongue, forget it, I —"

"But my main reason for calling," Patrick said, speaking loudly enough to override her words, "was that we've found what appear to be some valuable antiques in the cellar. I know you have an interest in such things, and I was hoping you'd come over to take a look at them and see if you think they're worth anything."

"Why, of course. I'd be delighted. Maybe I could look in on Rose, too, do you think so?"

"Yes, of course. May I speak to Amy now?" he asked somewhat abruptly, unwilling to drag out the conversation with his victim any further.

"You don't really have to if you don't want to, Patrick, your greatest fault is letting people like Amy impose on your good nature, you know. I'm sure —"

"I want to speak to her. Please."

"Oh, very well, but don't say I didn't try to protect you."

For the next few minutes he listened to a muffled quarrel between mother and daughter. Amy wanted Jane to leave the room while she spoke, but Jane resisted eviction. Patrick spent the time actively probing for Mordred's consciousness, something he wouldn't have dared to do before his recent victory. He could find no trace of him in his mind.

"Patrick? Are you still there?"

It surprised him that he was so pleased to hear her voice. He hadn't given her a thought since the night of the party. "Yes, Amy, how are you?"

She brushed aside routine civilities and asked: "Are you going to Dr. Ashcroft's Sabbat tonight?"

"Why —" he hadn't spared a thought for that since the party, either — "I don't know."

"Take me to it. *Please!*" She spoke with alarming passion. "I'm going, no matter what my mother says, but I'm a little bit scared to go there by myself, especially after what you told me. But I wouldn't be afraid if you were there. Won't you take me?"

The idea of a witches' Sabbat with people like Bob Bamberger in attendance now struck him as unutterably silly. Inside his own head he had a Master of the Runes who could teach him to raise the dead or destroy the living with a word. And no matter what promise he gave Amy now, it remained to be seen whether Mordred would let him attend the puerile charade.

"Patrick? You will take me, won't you?"

"I'd love to, Amy, but it's kind of difficult to make plans." He had to struggle not to laugh at his own lie, since it was not unlike the truth: "My grandparents, whom I haven't seen for a long time, are staying with us, and they may have planned something that I just can't get out of. And they aren't here just now, so I can't check with them. But if I possibly can, I'll take you."

"Oh, that's all right," she said, not trying to conceal her angry disappointment.

With no warning at all, Mordred returned and took possession of his voice, injecting it with lubricious insinuation: "Come now with your mother to visit me, sweet child, and we'll find ways to pleasure ourselves while she entertains my dear grandma."

Amy giggled. "You're in a weird mood."

"More weird than you can dream of, darling lamb. It is, after all, Hallowe'en, when a winsome girl like yourself should crave sweetmeats to suck upon."

"Maybe —" Amy began in a coy voice that was almost as suggestive as Mordred's, but she apparently thought better of whatever she had intended to say, and she finished briskly: "I'll come over."

— You are a milk-livered measle, Patrick. We could swyve that one in all her virginal holes without even troubling to cast a spell. But I see that you hold her in high regard, so we will not serve her as we did that Jennings strumpet. I am not the incarnate evil that you seem to believe, merely a man grown far older and wiser than the herd. You are beginning to understand that my presence can be a boon to you. It warmed me to feel the pride that you took in me.

Patrick winced, for that was true. Sneering at Ashcroft's party, he had indeed felt pride, like the keeper of an all-powerful secret. If Mordred would let him share in his power —

— I will indeed let you share. I will teach you all I know, I will let you command my strength, and in return you will direct your orderly intellect to our further studies. It may be that I do not need that heap of filth in the cellar, although she does know a thing or two that could ease our path. Your mind is as strong as hers, but you are not given to her sloth and viciousness.

Patrick listened, no longer bothering to raise a musical shield. The oily guile of Mordred's earlier tone was now absent from his mental voice. He sensed that Mordred was opening his own mind to him. He probed tentatively, still frightened of the pain that his ancestor could inflict, but he was not rebuffed. Soon they were communicating without words. He explored hidden chambers that held secrets of intolerable ugliness and chambers that held secrets of intolerable beauty. The one thing lacking in this vast and ancient mind was even the most rudimentary kind of organization. Patrick found himself compulsively tidying up, dusting off valuable bits and pieces of knowledge that Mordred had forgotten he possessed. At the same time he felt Mordred browsing in his own store of modern history and customs and colloquial speech. Patrick felt as if he were reading a vivid and exciting and challenging book; and as if, at the same time, the book were reading him.

He discovered one especially surprising fact: that it was Howard Ashcroft who had caused Mordred to rise from his slumber in Patrick's cellular memory. Although mostly a charlatan, Ashcroft commanded some magic that actually worked. He had used it in an effort to terrorize and confuse the Laughlins and force them to flee the mill. Ashcroft knew of Mordred's association with Dr. Dee and suspected that some material relevant to his studies in the *Necronomicon* might be concealed in the mill. Once he had gotten rid of the Laughlins, he had planned to dismantle the place in his search for it. His spells hadn't worked too well, but they had inadvertently set off powerful vibrations that had unleashed Mordred from his prison in the inherited chemistry of Patrick's body.

At first Mordred had been unable to communicate with him except in dreams, and then imperfectly. He had attempted to arouse his curiosity and his receptivity with visions of Mirdath. His efforts — characteristically careless and poorly focused — had affected others, too, inspiring Frank's pictures and Rose's breakdown. Before Patrick could even phrase the question, Mordred assured him that they could restore her to health easily enough: simply going far enough away from her would relieve the pressure of the vibrations that were exacerbating her condition.

Patrick was irked when the Miniters arrived, seemingly only minutes after he had hung up the phone.

"Sorry to take so long, Patrick, but I've been arguing with your devoted admirer, here," Jane said with a black look at Amy as he greeted them at the door, "and — no, Lance, *no!*"

Patrick crashed back against the wall as a black-and-rust bundle of muscle and fangs hurled itself against his chest. Jane and Amy grabbed the Doberman and wrestled him out the door before he could do any damage, then slammed it against him. All the dogs now took up the cry, flinging themselves at the door.

"What do you suppose has gotten into them?" Jane said, embarrassed and bewildered.

"Dogs have never liked me," Patrick muttered, angrily brushing at his sleeves.

"Since when?" Jane demanded. "You and Lance are old buddies."

He shrugged off the question, unable to answer. He had spoken as Mordred, whom dogs hated with a passion. Something odd and frightening had happened. In their shared moment of terror at the dog's attack, their identities had fused, so that it was no longer possible to say clearly who was who. The Mordred-part, as far as he could determine, was as frightened and angered by this development as the Patrick-part. This was not something the wizard had brought about or even desired.

"Amy said your grandparents are staying with you," Jane said, apparently reluctant to pursue the embarrassing subject of her dogs' behavior. She had to speak loudly to be heard over the clamor at the door. "They must be Frank's parents, right? I don't believe I've ever met them or even heard Rose or Frank speak of them, for that matter. Where are they now?"

"My grandmother is in the cellar at the moment. She's most eager to meet you." He laughed as he turned to lead the way through the house. "To use your phrase, you must be careful not to let her chew your ear off, as she hungers for human contact."

"And what's all this about antiques in the cellar?" Jane moved forward briskly to usurp the lead. "You aren't pulling my leg, are you? I thought Rose had explored this place from top to bottom when you moved in, but she never mentioned anything of that kind to me."

He ignored her prattle as he looked down at Amy. She smiled, but her smile wavered as his eyes lowered to make a survey of her slim young body. He reached out to caress her buttocks through her tight jeans. She jerked away in shock. But then she laughed and returned to his side. She didn't object when he slid his hand lower and caressed her even more intimately.

"What's all this about, Patrick?" she whispered. "Why did you really ask us to come here?"

"Well, first I'm going to feed your mother to the thing I keep in the cellar."

She giggled, rolling her eyes up. "You're nuts. Only I wish you really would. Then what?"

"And then, as you suggested the other night, I'm going to save you from a fate worse than death. Many times over."

She pulled away from his groping hand. Her face was flushed, her eyes shone. "You can. But only if you really feed my mother to the thing in the cellar."

He laughed wildly, and Jane, who had been talking volubly along some unnoticed course, turned to fix him with a shocked and angry stare.

"I don't find anything at all amusing about my late husband Arnold's death," she snapped.

"Perhaps you can right the balance then by dying an amusing death yourself. Would you care to lead the way with the flashlight?"

"He laughed at something I said, Mama. We weren't really listening to you. I'm sorry."

Jane's anger was defused, but she stared at each of them in turn with deep suspicion before she accepted the flashlight from Patrick and turned to descend the stairs. Amy tried to suppress a squeak when Patrick picked up the baseball bat that stood by the door.

"Grandma is in a foul mood," he whispered. "We must be prepared to defend ourselves."

"You *are* a nut. What is this, some kind of Hallowe'en joke?"

He merely nodded and chuckled as he followed Jane down the stairs, calling out to direct her. She walked to the indicated wall, then abruptly stepped back.

"It stinks down here! What on earth did you bring me down here to show me, antique sardines? And where's this grandmother of yours? Patrick, I'm beginning to seriously suspect that you're the one who ought to be under sedation. Where's Frank? I want to have a word with him."

"Calm yourself, Goodwife Miniter. There is a secret room here." He pressed the proper stones with the end of the bat. The door swung inward, freeing a gush of overwhelmingly fetid air. "Grandma! Lunchtime!"

With her hand over her nose, Jane stepped forward and shone the light into the depths. It dropped to the floor and went out as she screamed and screamed again. A deep, thudding sound with sucking, squishy overtones marked Mirdath's progress up the stairs. Amy tried to run, but Patrick circled her waist with his arm and held her fast. He felt a surge of exhilaration as he sensed that he and Mordred were no longer two people, but one. The fusion was now complete and seamless, with nothing that could be identified as a Patrick-part or a Mordred-part.

After outdoing all her previous efforts with one, ear-splitting shriek, Jane had stopped screaming. The only sounds now were the cracking and sucking noises that Patrick recognized from the night before.

"God, Patrick, what is it? What's happening? Mama! *Mama!*"

"Have you done stuffing yourself, then?" Patrick called. "If you've finished, return to the room while I quiff this squeaking poppet. Perhaps I'll let you have her soon, if she fails to please."

"I am going back to my grave," it said, and Amy shrieked at the sound of the gurgling, rasping voice that could never have been produced by a human throat.

Patrick laughed. "Back to your kennel, bitch! I will send you to your grave when I've done with you, not before."

"You are not my father," it stated in a tone he had not heard it use before.

Infuriated, he shouted: "I am more than your father, you nauseous obscenity! I am your father and your lover of old and your great-great grandson. I am the Master of the Runes! I am Patrick Glendower, Keeper of the Keys that are Yog-Sothoth!"

"You are not my father. And I still hunger."

Patrick took a step backward, still clinging to the shivering Amy. He was not afraid, but he was baffled and wrathful. He was more powerful than Mordred alone had ever been. He could control this blasphemy, he could blast it in its slimy tracks. He ransacked his mind for the appropriate words, but his mind had become infinitely vast, its store of information unmanageable. A bristly tentacle twined itself around his arm.

"Let me go, you filth!" he shrieked, releasing Amy to strike out with the bat and having the satisfaction of feeling it connect resoundingly. "Crawl back into your loathsome hole!"

He was wrenched forward with a force that rattled his teeth, slammed into the yielding putrescence of its torso. He raised the bat, but a chitinous mandible snapped it like a toothpick. In desperation he screamed the First of the Ten Words that are the Litany of Hastur. But in his ears howled the far more terrible Second Word.

Chapter Twelve

George Spencer braked his car sharply as he came to an unfamiliar gap in the woods surrounding the Laughlins' mill. Closer inspection showed that a swath two or three feet wide had been cut through the trees and underbrush. At the end he could see the mill itself, normally hidden from the road. The freshness of the splintered wood where the trees had been snapped off suggested a recent event. It looked as if someone had driven an uncommonly narrow bulldozer through the woods from the mill to the road.

He proceeded to the driveway, unable to keep his mind from dredging up an unpleasantly apposite reference in Lovecraft. In *The Dunwich Horror*, a similar but larger swath of destruction had marked the passage of an invisible monstrosity, the spawn of Yog-Sothoth and a mortal woman. He forced himself to accept the idea that a thoroughly conventional machine had made this one. Frank had decided to straighten his driveway, that was all.

Then he came to the house, and the balance tipped back in Lovecraft's favor. The door and its frame had been burst outward. Bloody pieces of dogs were strewn around the parking area. The dogs, together with the vaguely familiar vehicle that was parked here, suggested that Jane Miniter had become involved in the horror.

He rubbed his eyes wearily and lit a cigar before getting out and walking toward the house. Twenty years ago, Jane Miniter had been the prettiest girl in Mt. Tabor. He'd had a fling with her, his only deviation from fidelity to Madge. It was a great pity that she'd grown coarse and mannish in middle age. She had always babbled interminably, he reflected, but one doesn't always hold that against a desirable young woman. He recalled that he'd smuggled her along on one or two of his supposed literary excursions to Providence. The irony of that brought a bitter smile to his lips.

Around the house it was silent, utterly silent. Even the usually noisy crows seemed to have fled. The hint of a detestable odor hung in the still, damp air.

He recalled the odd item he had heard on the Willimantic radio station this morning. The news announcer had treated it lightly, but George paid it close attention, since it concerned the place where Rupert's car had been found abandoned. According to the newscast, some kind of upheaval had shaken the Mt. Tabor dump last night for a span of five minutes or so, like a minor and highly localized earthquake. Nearby residents reported that it had been accompanied by the release of an indescribably putrid stench. In the morning, what appeared to be a heap of newly disturbed rubbish and freshly dug earth was found near the center of the dump. It was suggested that gas, hydrogen sulfide or methane, imprisoned in a pocket of the rubbish, had erupted with some force.

Again his knowledge of Lovecraft provided him with an unsettling reference: "As a foulness ye shall know Them," he had written, purportedly quoting the *Necronomicon* on the subject of the Great Old Ones. But George suspected that the creature that had passed through here had been — at one time, anyway — mortal. Although God alone knew what its antecedents had been. The Old Ones could mate with mortals under the right circumstances, and perhaps that's why Patrick's ancestor had been concerned with concentrating his genetic heritage through incest.

He wished now that he had paid closer attention to what Rupert had told him about Patrick's interest in Mirdath's grave. He'd had all the necessary facts at his hand, but his obsession with that damned book had prevented him from putting them together in usable form. Patrick could have had only one reason for wanting to find Mirdath's grave. Rupert must have figured out Patrick's purpose, or perhaps he had noticed something unusual at the dump and entered it at just the wrong time George had toyed with the hope that he might still be alive, held prisoner in the mill to keep him from talking, but that slim hope had been dashed by the destruction he saw around him. He doubted that anything lived in the mill now.

He was reluctant to approach the building, but he forced himself to go forward. He might not have much time to find what he wanted. The mill was isolated, but the police would notice the swath cut to the road. They might just connect it to the incident at the dump and investigate. This was the only chance he might get to search the mill unobserved.

He approached the door warily. The odor grew stronger. He smiled wryly at his punctiliousness, but he pressed the button of the bell beside the ruined door.

As he had expected, no one responded to his ring. He stepped inside. Broken furniture and splintered walls marked the progress of the creature that had created the gap in the woods. He followed the trail through the huge room that the Laughlins called their Great Hall. A trail of a vile-smelling, tarry substance lay across the floor to the burst door of the kitchen.

In the kitchen, he saw that the cellar door had also exploded from its frame. He tried the cellar light-switch, but nothing happened. He spent ten minutes in a determined search for a flashlight. He eventually found a kerosene lamp, lit that, and descended steps thick with the tarry slime.

In the cellar he found a broken baseball bat, a crushed flashlight, and some shreds of clothing. He also found an assortment of human bones, although they were unaccountably translucent and rubbery. He descended to the secret room, where the odor was strongest and the black slime lay thickest on the floor. The table and chair had been splintered to matchwood, and many of the books had been shredded as if by a horde of rats. He sifted through the debris for a very long time, but he didn't find the book he wanted or any fragment of it.

Turning back up the stairs, he saw a pale figure standing above him. The light wavered as the lamp shook violently in his hand.

"Amy took some goodies to her grandma," Amy Miniter said in a wispy, sing-song voice, "but she had big eyes. And big teeth. And big claws."

"Now, now, Amy, it's all right," George said as he mounted the stairs slowly. "You're safe now. It's all over. You have nothing to fear."

"I told him to feed my mother to the thing in the cellar," she said, her voice breaking, "and he did. But it said it was still hungry, so it ate him. Then it looked for me. 'Come out, little girl,' it said. 'I won't hurt you.'"

He shivered at the reality of the voice suggested by her mimickry. He took her arm, but she pulled away.

"I let a boy touch me and my mother died," she said. "You can't touch me. Nobody will ever touch me again."

"I won't touch you, Amy. It's George Spencer. Don't you remember me?"

"Mama said she used to think you were the cat's pajamas." She giggled. "I could never look at you with a straight face, thinking what a funny pair of pajamas you'd make for a cat."

Maybe her laugh was a good sign, but she still seemed trapped in a four-year old perspective. It pained him to hear Jane's odd compliment from beyond the grave. "Come upstairs with me, Amy. You're cold, and I bet you're hungry, too."

"No! Grandma's upstairs. She's still hungry."

"It's gone back where it came from, Amy. It can't hurt you anymore. Look, follow me, I'll go first to prove it."

Amy followed. She seemed drawn by the lamp, as if she hungered for light even more than food after her ordeal. He convinced her to sit in the kitchen and found some milk and cookies for her. She stared at them queasily, as if she might throw up, but he hurried off to search the rest of the house. He saw that the viscous trail ran up the stairs. He sighed.

There was more to find.

He went directly to the top floor and Frank's studio, where the door had been smashed in. The shreds of an oil painting hung from the easel. Near it he found a rubbery thing that might once have been a human fibia. He tried to piece the tatters of the painting together, but it was beyond his powers of reconstruction.

He returned to the second floor. None of the doors there had been broken, but he checked behind them. He found Patrick's room. He entered and made a desultory examination of the bookshelves. He turned to the desk and tingled with shock at what he saw. For a moment, fearing disappointment, he dared not move closer to the fat volume that lay open on the desk. At last he approached it. He picked up the Dee translation of the *Necronomicon,* somewhat the worse for wear since he had seen it last. He hugged the massive book to his chest, squeezing his eyes shut against tears of happiness.

He hurried from the room. One door remained to be checked. He pushed it open without knocking.

"Why, George!" Rose sat up in bed and stared at him in bewilderment. "Is the party still going on? I. . . ." She looked around, noticed that it was day, and laughed. "I guess I really tied one on." She smiled ruefully. "The last thing I remember is talking to Dr. Ashcroft. Then, later in the night, it sounded as if someone was pushing a waterbed up and down the stairs outside my door. Isn't that silly? Was the party a success?"

"It was . . . delightful." He was at a complete loss to know how he should deal with her. She seemed quite herself, but he wondered how long her sanity would survive the revelations outside her bedroom door.

She laughed. "Why are you dressed like that on a Sunday morning, George? Don't you ever unwind? Oh — I'm sorry. I guess you've been to church, haven't you?"

He nearly let slip that it was Wednesday. He found himself staring at her with new and suspicious eyes, with a feeling verging on horror as he recalled his conjectures about the non-human strain in the Glendower heritage. He had never before noticed the almost batrachian protuberance of her large eyes, the reptilian sheen of her skin. He tried to brake his runaway imagination. He clutched the book more tightly. His only desire was to get out of here with it as quickly as possible.

Perhaps sensing his emerging hostility, she said sharply: "What are you doing here, George?"

"I came to borrow a book. Rose — I suppose I ought to tell you, it isn't Sunday. You've been unconscious for a couple of days. I think we ought to have Dr. Keller take a look at you before you try to get up."

She looked at him as if he had gone mad. "Where's Patrick? And Frank?"

"They've gone out." He drifted back toward the door. "I think the best thing for you is to lie here and let me call the doctor."

She got up and stood unsteadily for a moment, then collapsed back to the bed.

"I think you're right," she admitted. "Okay. But what happened to me? I certainly didn't drink *that* much."

"Food poisoning," he said with sudden inspiration. "A couple of other people were stricken, too. Nothing serious. But you'd better stay in bed until the doctor gets here."

"Oh, shit. Now I suppose we're going to be sued. You'll see us through it, won't you, George?"

"As a matter of fact, I've been planning to give up my practice," he said with a nervous laugh. "Devoting all my time to a hobby."

She looked at him oddly as he retreated to the door. She obviously hoped to quiz him further, but he could no longer deny his own burning curiosity. He gave her the briefest of farewells as he ran down the fouled stairs and out into his car. The doctor would look after her and Amy, too; his notable bedside manner had probably helped Mary Todd Lincoln stay calm.

Amy and Rose weren't his responsibilities. His duty lay to himself, who had found no answers to the great questions of life and had seen none of the wonders and terrors he had always dreamed of. His duty lay to Rupert, unfairly snatched away in the prime of his youth. All that could be made right. He hooked his reading glasses hastily to his ears and flipped impatiently through the book until a passage that he had skimmed the other day seemed to spring out at him.

"He who would be Master of the Runes," it read, "and Possessor of Life eternaille must consecrate to Crom Cruach on Lammas Night ye Flesh of an Infant newborn and eat thereof. Nor is the consecration to be made by those faint of heart or doubting in their souls, for Crom Cruach knows all, Crom Cruach sees all, Crom Cruach is all. Iä! Crom Cruach!"

Wondering when Lammas Night would fall next and where he might procure the necessary material, George closed his eyes and breathed, "Iä! Crom Cruach!"

He was rewarded with a sudden peal of unseasonable thunder that almost, but not quite, drowned out the screams coming from the mill.

About the Author

Brian McNaughton was born in Red Bank, New Jersey, and attended Harvard. He worked for ten years as a reporter for the *Newark Evening News* and has since held all sorts of other jobs while publishing some 200 stories in a variety of magazines and books. He recently ended a ten-year stint as night manager at a decrepit seaside hotel, where he once had the honor of helping his hero, Warren Zevon, break into a stubborn soda machine. *The Throne of Bones* won the World Fantasy and the International Horror Guild awards in 1998 for best collection.